THE MAKING OF THE NEXT GENERATION

BY EDWARD GROSS

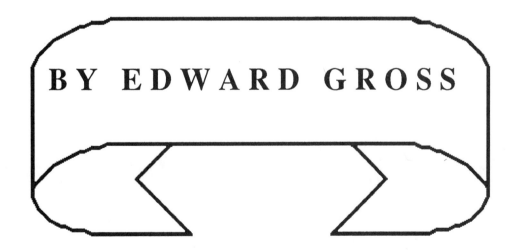

PIONEER BOOKS **LAS VEGAS, NEVADA**

A **PIONEER** TELEVISIONSHOWCASE BOOK
Series designed and edited by Hal Schuster

Library of Congress Cataloging-in-Publication Data
Gross, Edward,   1960—
   The Making of the Next Generation

   1. Star Trek: The Next Generation (Television program) I. Title
ISBN 1-55698-219-4

Published by Pioneer Books, Inc., 5715 N. Balsam Rd., Las Vegas, NV, 89130.
International Standard Book Number: 1-55698-219-4

First Printing 1989

INTRODUCTION

The adventure continues!

*That's the catch line that was introduced to the **Star Trek** universe with the release of **Star Trek: The Motion Picture** some ten years ago, and it seems more appropriate than ever as we celebrate the **Silver Anniversary of Star Trek.***

*Somehow it seems hard to believe that it's been 25 years since production of the first **Star Trek** pilot, "The Cage," but here we are, and there is more happening in that Gene Roddenberry-created world than ever before. For one thing, at the time of this writing, **Star Trek V: The Final Frontier** is little more than a month away from release. In addition, and bearing more of a relationship to the subject at hand, **Star Trek: The Next Generation** is in the midst of its second season, scoring the same high ratings as season one and continuing to prove itself to be one of the strongest television series in syndication. The characters, for the most part, are as strong as those featured in the old show and feature films, and the potential is there for this series to excel in terms of dramatic subject matter, provided that the creative staff push the limits of the medium as the original did.*

***The Making of The Next Generation** serves as an in-depth examination of the first season, analyzing (where possible) the genesis of each story from the concept stage to aired episode, and providing the viewpoints of the cast and crew who have labored to make the 24th Century a present day reality. This particular voyage should prove "fascinating" to fans of both the old show and the new, providing a look at the way a television series takes shape, and how it alters from the time of conception to that of broadcast.*

The adventure has just begun!

Edward Gross
May, 1989

PROLOGUE

t now seems obvious that **Star Trek** was destined to return to television. It is odd to remember that the show was a ratings disaster during its original run from 1966 to 1969, when Paramount Pictures considered it to be one of the all time biggest losers the studio had ever backed.

Corporate opinion began to change during the early 1970s when the series went into syndication and the now famous convention scene began. Suddenly more people were watching the show than ever before and thousands of them were gathering at these conventions to discuss the basic ideals presented by the series; to meet with the cast and crew who labored to bring the adventures of the starship Enterprise to the television screen; to

purchase memorabilia in an attempt to bring a piece of the show home with them. It was also during this time that *The Rumor* began: **Star Trek** would return! The difference between this rumor and others was that popular belief turned it into stark reality, albeit slowly.

Studying the phenomenon carefully, Paramount realized that they had *something* here; something undefinable, but surely something with a growing audience that a buck could be made from. The rumors circulated furiously that **Star Trek** would return as either a TV movie of the week, a new series, a feature film or a series of television movies. Finally, in 1973, it was announced that the show would return as an animated series to air on Saturday mornings. At first fandom wasn't impressed, but then it was learned that the original cast (except Walter Koenig) would be lending their vocal talents to their animated counterparts and that many science fiction veterans would be penning scripts for the show, including Dorothy Fontana, who also served as associate producer. This series lasted two seasons and produced 22 episodes, before slipping back into cancellation never-never land, and then syndication/video heaven.

The revival game began anew over the next few years with no less than three full-fledged theatrical attempts to get the project off the ground. Then, in June of 1977, Paramount announced that they would be starting a fourth network, the cornerstone of which was to be a new series entitled **Star Trek II**. The entire original cast, with the exception of Leonard Nimoy, was signed to play their familiar roles, new characters were added, numerous scripts and treatments were written, starship models were built and sets constructed. Then, one week before the commencement of production, the series was shelved, and Paramount announced that they would produce a multi-million dollar film, due, mostly, to 20th Century Fox's release of **Star Wars**, which would go on to become the most successful motion picture of all time.

Star Trek: The Motion Picture was released on December 7, 1979. Unfortunately, the production was chastised by just about everyone, from critics to the average moviegoer drawn in by the hype surrounding the film. The fans themselves were quite disappointed, but, despite this, the film did gross $175 million, thus paving the way for four sequels and a new television series.

When **Star Trek: The Motion Picture** was announced for production, there was a buzz of excitement concerning the choice of Robert Wise as director. His track record was impressive, with such credits as **West Side Story**, **The Sound of Music**, **Cat People** and, of course, **The Day the Earth Stood still**. He was a distinguished film-maker, and it seemed likely that he would bring forth a vision of **Star Trek** unlike any that had been presented before.

At the same time, there was a concern that Wise, a relative stranger to **Star Trek**, would have problems dealing with a cast who had a considerably better grasp of their characters than he did. Still, he attempted to overcome this potential hurdle by producing what he hoped would be the ultimate cinematic voyage into outer space.

In many interviews, the director stated that he took on the project because it presented the opportunity to enter space, whereas his other genre experiences had been Earth-bound. Bearing this in mind, it's easier to understand why he took the approach he did.

Looking back at **Star Trek: The Motion Picture**, it is very easy to see that it was a failed attempt to create a latter day version of Kubrick's **2,001: A Space Odyssey**, with slow sweeps of space and overwhelming attention devoted to special effects. Unfortunately such an approach could seem little more than tedious for modern audiences, because **Star Wars** had altered expectations of what science fiction could do on screen. Wise tried to update and alter the public's perception of **Star Trek**, but in so doing he lost the humanity of the basic premise that had appealed to viewers in the first place.

Although the film did eventually turn a profit, there was still doubt as to whether there would be a sequel. It had gone nearly disastrously over budget and Paramount was adamant that the situation not occur again. They eventually did decide to do a follow-up, and a search began for a director who could keep the film on schedule and within budget. Nicholas Meyer was chosen.

Meyer's approach to what was eventually subtitled **The Wrath of Khan** was to act as though there had been no **Star Trek** adventures before it. His intention was to make the film accessible to the average moviegoer as well as the fans, rather than catering primarily to the latter.

As had become his trademark, Meyer did his part in making the characters from the TV show breathe with a life of their own, with the underlying theme of aging and mortality playing an important role. He took into account the passage of years between the film and the last episode of the television series, and had the characters reflect on the past. This was in direct contrast to the first film's attempt to keep the characters exactly as they had been ten years earlier. In this **Star Trek** universe you believed that people would die and *not* come back (although the next sequel would negate that).

The news that Meyer would not helm **Star Trek III: The Search For Spock** was disappointing, although unsurprising considering his dislike for sequels. Bearing this in mind, however, it does seem strange that he co-wrote the screenplay for **Star Trek IV: The Voyage Home**, but who's to argue?

More than a few eyebrows were raised when Paramount announced that Leonard Nimoy would be calling the shots on the new film. Yes, he certainly knew and understood the material and had earned quite a few television directorial credits, but could he make the transition to the motion picture screen, particularly on a film with such a large budget and so many special effects? And what would his fellow cast members think?

Wasn't this intergalactic nepotism?

Mr. Nimoy surprised many with his directorial skills on **The Search For Spock**. Not only did the film work, it worked quite well. The third entry in the series was a winner, falling slightly behind the second and light years ahead of the first. Nimoy had changed tactics from Meyer, deciding that it was okay to appeal primarily to Trekkies, *if* the film truly represented the original television series. If the average moviegoer wanted to check up on the Enterprise crew, that would be okay too, but the film was filled with so much Trek lore that no one but fans would be able to completely follow what was going on.

Nimoy returned as director of **The Voyage Home**, which also catered to fans, but, with a high humor content, had a very strong universal appeal, helped immeasurably by a story set in our own time period. Time travel had been dealt with several times on the original series, but, with the exception of "City on the Edge of Forever," none had been as effective as this. The clash of cultures between "them" and "us" rivals anything found in either **Back to the Future** or **Peggy Sue Got Married**.

William Shatner has directed **Star Trek V: The Final Frontier**, and his approach has been to marry the humor of its predecessor with the action and suspense of **Aliens**, as the starship Enterprise sets off on its latest mission: to encounter God.

By the mid nineteen eighties, it seemed that **Star Trek** would "live out" the rest of its years on the silver screen. Yet despite the success of the films, rumors began anew several years ago concerning a spinoff television series. One story had it that Paramount approached the networks about reviving the series, while another had CBS, NBC, ABC and Fox Broadcasting coming to the corporation and requesting the show. Of the networks, this story stated, it seemed likely that the show would go to either ABC or Fox, although the latter seemed the best choice. The reason for this is simple, and it dates back to the days of **Star Trek**'s original run when, as was pointed out earlier, the show was never a ratings winner. Its demographics, conversely, were incredibly strong and because of this it might have a better chance on a network without much concern for Neilson ratings. Such a move would have undoubtedly freed the show to tackle virtually any subject without fear of undue censorship and, conceivably, could have led to a higher quality show .

Another suggestion was that perhaps there would be a new cast of characters, with cameos by members of the original ensemble. However, after a while just about everyone brushed these stories off as rumors, with no foundation in fact to support them. In the meantime, Paramount, the public and the media prepared for the September 1986 20th Anniversary of the original series. Then the bombshell was dropped: **Star Trek** would indeed be returning to television via syndication. The name of the series would be **Star Trek: The Next Generation**, and it would be produced for syndication by Gene Roddenberry, who had been guaranteed complete creative control over the show.

Over the next few months, news came out slowly, but emphasized that the new series would have nothing to do with the original show, that there would be no descendents of Kirk and Spock, that the Klingons were now allies and that the show would be much less militaristic than the original or the feature films. In addition, the setting would be about seventy five years beyond the last (now known as "classic") Trek.

In the beginning, numerous people from the original series were involved with the creation of **The Next Generation**, including David Gerrold, Dorothy Fontana, Eddie Milkis, John D.F. Black and Robert Justman. Of them, only Justman would make it through the first season, with the others leaving the show, or being asked to leave, over creative differences. The specific reasons for these departures is a story best told elsewhere. In this book we are exploring only the episodes themselves, and their creative genesis.

SECOND PROLOGUE

*The following interviews were conducted with the entire cast of **Star Trek: The Next Generation** shortly after the airing of the premiere episode, "Encounter at Farpoint." The interviews were written by Mark A. Altman, from the efforts of Altman himself, Steven Simak and Mitchell Rubinstein. These interviews, as well as the set-visit chronicle which appears in this chapter, are reprinted with the kind permission of **Galactic Journal** magazine.*

PATRICK STEWART:

the man who

would be captain

"I think it is high time that I became involved in some action," Patrick Stewart laughs as he reclines in front of his trailer during a break in shooting the latest episode of **Star Trek: The Next Generation**. "I'm somewhat of a sedentary character and since Riker leads the away teams, he's having all the fun."

Stewart, one of Great Britain's most well respected thespians, has in only several weeks immortalized the character of Captain Jean Luc Picard in the minds of television fans across the country. His other recent works have included **Smiley's People** and **Tinker, Tailor, Soldier, Spy** for the BBC as well as essaying the roles of Gurney Halek in **Dune** and Leondegrance in John Boorman's **Excalibur**. He most recently starred in a London production of "Who's Afraid of Virginia Woolf," for which he was the recipient of the prestigious London Fringe Best Actor Award.

"It's been my lot for years to play a whole list of national leaders, dictators, kings, princes and party bosses and I've never found that tiresome," he affirms. "For one thing, if you play a king you get to sit down a lot when other people are standing. In this series, it tends not to work out that way. I tend to be on my feet all the time."

Pondering the subtext of Picard, Stewart confesses to a fascination with the use of power which is such an essential part of the character's success. "I am truly interested as a human being and as an actor in the use of power; how it is acquired and how it works. I've always been quite a political person and I've always been fascinated with the use of power in politics.

"It was always important to me to try and establish and affirm the quiet, but absolute, authority he has on the ship, and that seems to be successful. The letters I have received have talked about the authority of the captain; that he is truly a commander, and that's important, because if you don't

have that as an actor playing the role, you're drowning from day one."

While the characters who Stewart has played in the past have wielded power differently and utilized it for incongruous ends, it is an aspect which has characterized a large body of his work. In addition, as Stewart readily notes, the structure of **Star Trek** is something he felt at home with as well. "There is truly a classic form to each **Star Trek** story. They have a shape that is exactly in the mold of classic theatre. So in that sense and in the slightly epic nature of the characters, was something that was familiar to me. But at the same time, I must be careful not to make that in any way two-dimensional."

Stewart discards the notion of television as an inferior medium and points to its tremendous impact on society as warranting serious consideration. "It's a medium that has to be taken very, very seriously now. Television, in every area of our lives, is probably the most potent, whereas how many people does the theatre touch? I'm told we played to over two million people in the Greater Los Angeles area last Sunday night. That's more people than I've played to in a lifetime while acting on stage."

JONATHAN FRAKES:

he's number one

"I think the costumes look great, but I'm not really crazy about wearing thick spandex," confesses Jon Frakes, who plays the heroic and stoic William Riker, as he lounges around his trailer in a radiant pink bathrobe. "I like Riker...a lot. I've played a lot of sleazy shitheads, so it's nice to play a hero."

Frakes admits to a bit of trepidation over inheriting the mantle of a legendary television series, but it was a challenge he approached with great enthusiasm. "There was a lot of skepticism and there was a high potential for failure. There have also been a lot of comparisons with Shatner. I'll take his career; he's quite good. The comparisons are inevitable. If they're positive, that's fine. The differences between the two series are so cut and dry, yet the quality has stayed the same."

In the Sixties, it was often difficult to draw the distinction between Shatner's on-screen persona and Shatner himself. The same could be said for Frakes and his alter-ego, Riker. While Frakes is more relaxed and humorous, he shares many traits with his celluloid creation and, as a result, is interested in seeing him develop in a manner consistent with his own ideals. "I'd like to see the character have a little more fun; he's really the most stable and straight-laced of the lot. I'd like to go backwards in time to Dixieland, New Orleans and to approach subjects and see what they would be like in the 24th Century, such as sports and the arts. Now, with the holodeck on the ship we can go and be anywhere.

"I'm looking forward to developing more of the romance with Troi," he adds, hinting about future romantic entanglements with the attractive Betazoid counselor. "That has sort of been on the backburner lately, but it is an element that needs to be played up. I think it's a good idea to keep that approach/avoidance thing. I think it's titillating to an audience. It certainly worked on **Cheers** and **Moonlighting**. I like that stuff. It's fun."

Among the episodes Frakes cites as his favorites are "Aida," a farcical chapter in the Enterprise saga, and "The Big Goodbye," a show which places Riker, Captain Picard, Data and Dr. Crusher in a 1940s Chandler-esque detective yarn while trapped on the holodeck. "I spend a lot of time in period costume in that one. I liked in the old **Star Trek** when they beamed down in suits; anything to get out of this costume."

Frakes numbers playing the trombone as one of his most passionate interests, along with acting and ponders whether it is a pursuit he will be able to develop on the road. "I hope I will eventually get to play the trombone...somewhere. I could be in a Dixieland Band or in **Star Trek**...this pays better. Roddenberry's vision of the future is also so positive; that there's not going to be a nuclear war and we'll go on and improve the quality of life. It's not a bad way to spend your day."

BRENT SPINER:

data entry

"Assuming the show goes six years, I think my character is on a journey towards humanity," says Brent Spiner, the Pinnochio of the new **Star Trek** series. "He is a character who is growing because he's amongst humans. I think of him as being very young in terms of how long he's been existing, so there's a childlike quality; a naivete and a wide-eyed acceptance of everything going on around him."

Spiner, who has numerous Broadway stage credits to boast of (but doesn't), accepts the comparisons with his illustrious predecessor as the Enterprise's science officer, but draws some important distinctions. "The similarity is in the factual area; information, logic, etc. In every other way, we're complete opposites. I long to be human and he had no interest in even recognizing his own humanity." Spock, of course, was half-human while Data is not.

Pondering the thought of seeing a replica of himself in the hands of excited little children on Christmas morning (and Chanukah evening) is a thought that stirs mixed emotions in Spiner. "I'm not the most high-profile person, but all of that stuff is really part of it all. If I ever feel weird about it, I think Harrison Ford and Alec Guinness had action figures, so if it's good enough for them, it's good enough for me."

Playing an android is an unenviable task for an actor who has to follow in the footsteps of a myriad of spectacular screen android performances. Spiner approached the role from a different perspective. "I sort of just had to start with what was in the script and what was available for me from myself. I didn't see **Making Mr. Right** because I was afraid I would like what John Malkovich was doing and want to go towards it. My interpretation is as valid as anyone else's as to what an android is going to be like in the 24th Century."

The soft-spoken actor readily admits doing convention appearances is not his cup of tea. "I'm not one for going out into public and saying this is who I really am, and destroying this illusion for you that I've been trying to create all year long."

LEVAR BURTON:

guiding the way

LeVar Burton may be fun loving and amiable on the set with his peers, but when it comes down to talking shop about his craft, he turns completely serious. Burton's worked hard to get where he is. He knows it, and wants you to know it too. Among his previous works Burton can boast of the hit miniseries **Roots**, the experimental dramatic TV movie **Emergency Room** and the highly acclaimed children's show, **Reading Rainbow**.

Now he's portraying the blind navigator of the Enterprise, Geordi La-Forge, and he's damn happy about it.

"I find that this fits well into my plans and my career," Burton remarks, speaking softly but firmly. "I have always, above all else, wanted to do good work and **Star Trek** is certainly an opportunity to do good work."

His affinity for the character is apparent, although he readily points out if he were playing another character he would find all of the things about that character that he liked. "I like Geordi for a lot of reasons. First of all, his energetic attitude is much more loose than that of a lot of the other characters. He is very loose and speaks his mind. He has a sort of cynical sense of humor and I like that about him. I like the opportunity to play a character who is handicapped, yet that handicap has been turned into a plus for him and there are all the emotional issues that go along with that."

As for the future development of the character, Burton is more reticent and unwilling to put himself in the shoes of the writers. "I've had several conversations with the producers and with Gene, and now that I'm here, they really want to make use of me and they're working on it. I'm being patient and letting them do their job and trusting them that their word is as good as their bond. It's a creative process that involves more than just me and what I want for the character. There are certainly many other people who have input in the decision making in terms of where this character goes. I'm very happy that they respect my opinion and ask for it, but just in terms of the future development of Geordi, it's like throwing pebbles in a pond. It has ripples and repercussions. My job is to come and do my work every day and be patient."

For Burton, unlike many of the other cast members, **Star Trek** is only another facet of a prestigious and continually evolving career which has spanned the last decade. It is a job he takes seriously and, in his opinion, demands respect. "I love this job. I love the opportunities to do these stories with this group of actors, producers and writers and to provide entertainment that also makes you think once in a while. That's what I built a career on and I'm really happy to be able to do it in this framework."

DENISE CROSBY

keeping the enterprise secure

Denise Crosby's come a long way since that classic high-camp moment in "Encounter at Farpoint" where she admonishes Q from the floor of his council chamber: "You should get on your knees to Starfleet!" Since then, good old Tasha's been abducted by Legonites, launched a fair share of photon torpedoes and recalled visions of the rape gangs which roamed her savage planet.

In describing Tasha, Crosby is the first to admit there is a lot more to the character than meets the eye. "The emotional side of Tasha intrigues me as well as her feminine conflicts and being able to establish relationships with people in a trusting way. She's never had that; there's no history of that in her life. There's no family; there's no love."

Among the stories Crosby is particularly interested in seeing occur are those that would involve aspects of human behavior. "I would like to see a kind of romance happen with her where she has that conflict of career and romance. Basically, we're all open to that that kind of thing. It's human interest stories, not just the story of babbling aliens."

Crosby is intent on creating a unique character with depth who fans will find appealing, not just one that fulfills Gene Roddenberry's vision of a watered down Jenette Goldstein. "They originally envisioned Tasha as more butch. I think Tasha is reflective of women's roles and what they're trying to achieve at this point.

In the Sixties, there really weren't too many roles like this. There were things, for instance, like **Julia**, in which Dianne Carroll played a single working mother living on her own and I think that was revolutionary. If you look back at that, it was incredible. It was amazing, because women were very much struggling with being pregnant in the workforce and trying to raise kids as they still are."

Tasha's distinct multi-faceted personality ranges from the hands-on security chief to the voluptuous vixen which was unleashed in "The Naked Now." Crosby notes, "What I like about this character is she's strong physically and direct, and is comfortable with who she is. I envisioned Tasha as what I brought to it. I sort of like the quality there that she could be attractive and sexy, and still be able to kick the shit out of anyone."

MARINA SIRTIS:

if i could read your mind

"I got recognized in the car park...even with dark glasses on," says Marina Sirtis excitedly. Unlike her on-screen counterpart, Counselor Deanna Troi, Sirtis is a bubbly Brit whose personality bears more of a resemblance to Tracy Ullman than the blushing Betazoid.

Sirtis, who radically transformed her character after the pilot, has undergone the most dramatic character metamorphosis in the series so far. "We felt that the character was a little too intense. There wasn't enough range in Troi. All she seemed to be feeling was a lot of anguish and as an actress it would have gotten real boring after two episodes. I watched the pilot with my hand over my eyes. I didn't feel it was working really well.

"If you are telepathic, a psychologist and hugely super intelligent, she would be so understanding, so nice, so forgiving and laid back, she would be the Linda Evans of **Star Trek**. What we want is a little more of the Alexis," Sirtis affirms, alluding to the ABC soap opera **Dynasty**. "I've worked more on developing the human side of her. That's far more interesting to play because she's half human. Human beings are interesting and quirky. The old **Star Trek** episodes which were really fascinating were where Spock's guard dropped or he felt something, not the totally Vulcan thing."

Sirtis is thrilled with being a part of the **Star Trek** phenomena, although she acknowledges her fear of failure in the beginning. "If you look up actress in the dictionary, it says insecurity. This was my Hollywood dream. There's pressure, but it makes me feel really good. The bad part is when you can be knocked down. If it didn't work out, we were going to be destroyed. We're good actors, though, and it's a good show."

One of Sirtis' favorite episodes is "Haven," because of its ironic echoing of a real life experience she had in her own family. "It's an arranged marriage kind of situation and being Greek, my parents tried to do that to me once. The relationship between me and my mother on the show [Majel Barrett] was so similar to the feelings of me and my mother. I worked harder on that episode than I've ever worked on anything in my life."

Among her two most difficult acting challenges are working with props and the dreaded shaking action when the ship is struck by phaser fire or any mysterious force. "We point our phasers and nothing happens. When you see it, this magic blue light comes out. I don't ever have any props though. They tried to shove some props at me, but I said I'm the mental character. I don't use all that stuff. I don't like using it, because if you can drop it or break it, I will drop it or break it.

"I'm not adept at the shaking action either," she laughs. "I thought everybody shook better than me. I can't take it seriously, maybe because I'm British. The Americans shake and do it really well and I'm on the floor doubled over with laughter. If my drama teachers could see me now, they would die."

Sirtis, whose American Visa was rapidly expiring when she got the role, admits to a passion about her vocation and her role in the ensemble cast of **Star Trek** despite the 17 hour days and hectic shooting schedules. "I've always said I act for free. They pay me for waiting around."

GATES MCFADDEN

good health comes first

Gates McFadden never considered becoming a Pre-Med when she went to Brandeis University in exciting Waltham, MA in the early 1970s. "I'd rather just slip right into the position at the hospital without the Pre-Med," she jokes. She could have hardly expected to find herself aboard the bridge of the starship Enterprise tending frozen crewmembers, stricken space travellers and the like, but, of course, that's exactly where she is, portraying Dr. Beverly Crusher, the Enterprise's Chief Medical Officer and mother of the brilliant Wesley Crusher.

"I think it would be interesting to see the women have more relationships," McFadden reveals about her hopes for the future development of the show. "That's an area to explore. I am also fascinated with what medicine is like in the 24th Century. Do you do laser surgery? What sort of care does one get? Especially nowadays when you're talking about the depersonalization of medical care and how difficult hospital stays are. Illnesses are changing and people can linger now for years with a debilitating disease. I am interested in delving into issues like that, because I find it fascinating."

Having taught and participated in experimental theatre for years, the role of a pop icon seems like an unlikely one for McFadden, but it is one she fulfills admirably. "It is an ensemble show and I like the other people who were cast. I felt the producers really wanted me to be a part of it and it was nice to be wanted. I was also impressed with Gene Roddeberry.

"I've had many comments from people who would reinforce the position that we are not just another evening soap," McFadden states vehemently. "There are some philosophical points of view that are presented and that's always going to be part of it."

Some of McFadden's most impressive accomplishments were her involvement with the behind-the-scenes execution of two of Jim Henson's most impressive and ambitious projects, **Labyrinth** and the fantasy segments of **Dreamchild**. A mutual friend had recommended McFadden as a choreographer to Henson, who had already cast her in a small roll in is film **The Muppets Take Manhattan**. "I was doing something in Woodstock when he called and said, 'I have this movie **Dreamchild**. Can you fly over and do it?' I had already done some stuff for him, so I flew over, he briefed me for an hour and took off. He's definitely a baptism by fire guy. I was doing something I had never done in my life; rehearsed a week, shot a week and was done."

MICHAEL DORN:

for battle, come to me

"This guy is about power and strength," Michael Dorn, the man under the make-up, reveals about the first Klingon Starfleet Academy graduate. "All the other characters have a certain softness, except Tasha, so it's a complement. The character is proud of his heritage and proud of his record. This guy's a madman, but he's extremely loyal to his ship and his crew. I use my voice a lot; it's a lot deeper and gone deeper since the shows have gone on."

Reflecting on Klingon heritage, Dorn doesn't find their newfound alliance with the Federation all that unacceptable. "Klingons weren't exactly evil as they were totally aggressive. I approached it with that attitude. They liken it to after World War II and how the Japanese and the Americans worked so closely together. Bitter enemies were working together, and citizens in each country. That's taking a page right out of history. Also, us and the Russians. You have to have your head in the sand not to believe sooner or later we're going to be friends...or, at least, allies."

In preparing to play Worf, Dorn notes that he was not influenced by any of the other classic **Star Trek** Klingon performances. "You knew who they were. You looked at Kruge, and said, 'That's Christopher Lloyd,' or Michael Ansara, who was playing himself and saying, 'We need no urging to hate humans.' That's their thing. With my character, because I'm not well known, I can build it from the ground up. I can make my character totally different and a lot deeper.

"I'd love to have a story where he meets someone from his past," Dorn says, pondering Worf's future adventures. "Either a family member or a love interest—which is always interesting."

Dorn points to "Justice" as one of his favorite episodes. "We were on a planet of lovemakers, and there were some great lines that had to do with me and sexuality. I like the ones with a touch of comedy. The fun stuff is what I really enjoy, although the action is always fun. He's always been right in the middle of the battles and fight scenes."

Of all the cast members, next to Wil Wheaton, Dorn is probably the biggest **Star Trek** aficionado, so the opportunity to participate in the saga was particularly exciting. "I said to my agent that I wanted to get on the show somehow. When you get the call, the actor takes over and you have to approach it as just another job. I got the part, I got all excited. If I hadn't gotten it, I figured I could always guest star..."

WIL WHEATON

pecocious ensign

"It is new to me to play a very smart kid," says Wil Wheaton, the new kid on the **Star Trek** block, literally. "I've always played the nice, down to earth guy, so Wesley is a big change for me."

Wheaton, though, is well aware of the child genius syndrome which can alienate an audience, such as Robbie Rist's annoyingly inept Dr. Z in **Galactica 1980,** and is anxious to avoid it. "He's precocious, but not intentionally. Our characters are like our alter-egos, so I don't want to see an episode where Wes turns into a brat, because it's not true to the character. I don't want to see him become the ultimate brain or the stupid little kid. Wes is in the position where he is a teenager with the intellect of an adult. It's not his fault, but he likes it and doesn't try to prevent his intellect from showing. A lot of times it will come across as smart ass, but he doesn't mean it."

The critically acclaimed actor admits to an intense affinity for **Star Trek** and is well aware he's living out every Trek fan's dream. "This is a big deal for me, because I'm a Trekkie. I love the show. It's sort of like the kid who always wanted to be President and is in the White House and gets to meet the President. When I was a kid, I never thought someday I could be in **Star Trek.**"

As a fan who's anxious to keep up with all the latest **Trek** memorabilia, Wheaton devours all the latest books, comics and technical manuals. "I justify my purchases of any **Star Trek** items as a business expense. I'm researching my character, thank you very much...write that off."

Wheaton particularly relishes the thought that **Star Trek V** may be shooting at the same time as **Star Trek: The Next Generation**, assuming the series is renewed for a second season. "I'll get to meet Captain Kirk, Spock, McCoy, Chekov and Uhura." For the moment though, Wil Wheaton couldn't be happier.

"My two passions are surfing and acting. Surfing I can only do at the beach when the waves are okay. Acting I can do every morning and get to work with these wonderful people. It's a learning experience. There's no such thing as the actor who knows everything, because everyday you learn something new. I act because I want to. Almost all of the very dedicated actors act because they want to. Everyone on our show is here because they want to be here—they love acting."

THIRD PROLOGUE

"You couldn't imagine how hard it is to get on the back of a box of Cheerios," the publicist representing **Star Trek: The Next Generation** explained to me as he pointed at the back of a cereal box. On it was a picture of a young boy flanked by Jonathan Frakes and Marina Sirtis. In the starfield above them it said you could win a chance to appear in a **Star Trek** episode, and at the very least you could find a sticker with your favorite **Next Generation** star inside. I nodded. It was hardly what anyone would have expected when the cameras first started to roll on the pilot for **Star Trek** way back in 1965, but now, over twenty years later, history was being made again, not only on the airwaves, but in kitchen cabinets across America as well.

I put the box back down on the table next to the water cooler. On the other side of the plywood wall separating us was the bridge of the new Enterprise, where rehearsal was beginning on another scene in the latest episode of the critically acclaimed new syndicated space opera.

"You will jump to warp eight and I will personally lead the Away Team," says one of the episode's guest stars as he struts down to the helm. Patrick Stewart rises from the captain's chair and walks to the ops position and turns. Rob Bowman, the director, shakes his head disapprovingly. He approaches Stewart, they exchange hushed words and all is well again. Stewart and LeVar Burton exchange quips and they prepare to rehearse the scene again. Denise Crosby, who plays Security Chief Tasha Yar, looks somewhat out of place in back of the weapons console in a white halter top as she does her make-up. The cast patiently awaits for the scene to be rehearsed again.

It is here, on Stage 10, that the bridge of the Enterprise is housed along with the captain's ready room and several of the principal personnel quarters. Several soundstages down is Stage 9, where most of the permanent sets for the series are housed. Most are re-dressed versions of the motion picture sets. The scarred remnants of the battle bridge featured in "Encounter at Farpoint" is now substituting for the USS Stargazer, Captain Picard's former command, and was the original bridge from **Star Trek: The Motion Picture**. Nearby is sickbay, the multipurpose briefing room, the transporter room and engineering. All the gadgets adorning the **Trek** sets have been carefully thought out and are engineered to operate in a certain way.

"The art department have programmed all that stuff," Denise Crosby says. "They know exactly what all of it does. All you have to do is say what does this thing do or how would I launch a photon torpedo? They have all that worked out."

Adjacent to engineering and through one of the myriad Enterprise deck corridors is an all-purpose area which will eventually serve as the ship's shuttlecraft bay, if need be. It is currently used for storage and was uti-

lized for the holodeck sequence in "Code of Honor".

The holodeck, an exciting new piece of Enterprise technology, was first envisioned during the animated **Trek** episodes, but has been vividly realized in the new series. It will play a vital part in upcoming **Trek** stories, reveals Jonathan Frakes, who plays the new Enterprise's first-in-command and away team leader, William Riker. "Brent and I went on location in the Ferndale area for the holodeck," Frakes notes of its use in "Encounter at Farpoint". In the scene, he encounters Data in the wilds of a Terran forest. It was some of the only location shooting that the series would feature until "Justice", otherwise known as the Edo Planet episode. Rob Legao, who's responsible for the series visual effects, has found the holodeck sequences some of his most challenging work. "It's all a heavy blue screen composite. He [Frakes] is actually walking on a blue screen floor. We try to keep all the shadows as they actually appear on the floor so they will appear on the exterior location so it looks like he's married to it. It's a fairly complex composite."

The holodeck is the catalyst for a Raymond Chandler-esque episode which both Frakes and Gates McFadden cite as one of their favorite adventures yet. In "The Big Goodbye," written by Tracy Torme, the holodeck malfunctions, trapping our heroes in a dangerous fantasy world.

Nearby on Stage 16, a bulldozer is sitting idle as workers scurry across the huge soundstage in which styrofoam rocks appear to stretch into the horizon. The set is used for creating

23

alien terrains and also houses an underground area which can be flooded, if necessary.

"We did it the same way we did it twenty years ago," explains Supervising Producer Robert Justman, one of the veterans from the original **Trek**. "We have a slightly larger stage this time, but it's much the same idea. He adds that there will be a "50/50 mix of planet to ship shows."

The man endowed with the thankless task of creating **Star Trek**'s alien worlds is Production Designer Herman Zimmerman, who, in conjunction with a varying tinting and lighting scheme, is charged with transforming Stage 16 every week into a totally new planetary environment. "Production design and art design is problem solving," Zimmerman states. "Problem solving with an intent. I like to say that the art director/production designer is in the unenviable position of making himself invisible. Because if what he or she does is correct, it supports that story; it becomes the environment. If what he does becomes visible to you, then he's probably stepped out of line and you are noticing the technique of the matte painting denoting an alien landscape, rather than believing you are there on an alien landscape."

Back on Stage 10, filming has begun. Captain Picard is attempting to console the wife of a Starfleet ambassador whose husband has been taken hostage by terrorists. The set is quiet as the cameras begin to roll.

Outside the cramped soundstage is a small trailer court, housing all the principal cast. Extras lounge around in front of the soundstage door, while Marina Sirtis' make-up is being applied as the Beatles blare loudly from a portable radio. Jonathan Frakes pops out from his trailer in his pink bathrobe to see when he's needed on stage in costume again and then retreats back into his trailer, and out of the hot California sun. Wil Wheaton is bouncing around the set, even though he won't be appearing in any scenes that day. LeVar Burton is inside his trailer, appearing to be having some very serious conversations with his agent as Michael Dorn reclines in a patio chair outside his humble **Star Trek** chateau.

Old is indeed new again, even if the next generation of crew members of the Starship Enterprise are part of an all-new **Star Trek** that has changed more than just the faces at the helm.

"The way we do the show nowadays is different physically," Robert Justman explains. Unlike the old **Star Trek** series, **The Next Generation** is shot on film, but transferred to one inch video for editing. "We've never seen an inch of positive film." The only shooting in which positive film is screened is for certain effects shooting. Processes such as optical printing are eliminated through the new method which not only allows for a higher resolution picture quality, but eliminates the degraded image which results from the various generations film stock would go through before airing.

The show's visual effects are composited digitally as well so several elements can be combined into one shot more easily than through traditional optical printing methods. "We can take Vista Vision film from ILM and 35mm film from somewhere else, and marry them all digitally," Justman adds. The episodes, once edited, are beamed by satellite to the independent stations across the country who carry the show.

While the method of production has changed dramatically from the original, other obstacles to recreating the **Trek** universe were less easy to surmount. Among the dilemmas Production Designer Herman Zimmerman had to face was being faithful to the original **Star Trek** concepts established in the series and the movies, and improving on them. "We still have a double warp drive engine, we still have impulse power, use the transporter room and have a bridge with the captain in the center," says Zimmerman. "All of those things are generic to what we know and believe **Star Trek** to consist of. While we are upgraded in details and cosmetics, we are alike in kind and that's not so hard to do. If we were reinventing the wheel, that would be hard. Why tamper with success?

"There was a desire to come across with a new Enterprise in a spectacular way. In the case of the new Enterprise, it's twice the size of the last Enterprise, which was considerably larger than the first television Enterprise. The concept from Mr. Roddenberry was not to deviate, in essence, from the philosophy of the original.

"The new bridge design evolves as does the exterior ship design from two basic concepts. One is it is unnecessary to have aerodynamics because space is a vacuum. It is, by the 24th Century, in Mr. Roddenberry's mind, entirely possible that technology has reached such a state of proficiency that it has become an art form.

Point two is that instead of a five year mission, we have a 30 year mission with women, children and families aboard. We want to make the whole environment of the starship more comfortable. It never was a battleship. It's a far cry from an all grey militaristic starship. It is indeed a state of the art, comfortable machine that we're proud to call home."

One of the most important facets of designing the new Enterprise was the bridge, which has undergone a dramatic evolution since the original television series. "The bridge is large," Zimmerman remarks. "Perhaps larger than it needs to be, partly because Gene wanted the viewscreen to be very large. It's considerably more advanced looking than the original Enterprise viewscreen, and it lends a great deal of dramatic impact to the shows when you can see the face of Q, for instance, nine feet high in front of Picard, who is standing there a little more than half that height."

The construction of such a large viewing screen demanded that the rest of the bridge be built to a scale which would be compatible with it. The bridge, in fact, is the same width as the original Enterprise bridge—38 feet—but is two feet longer. The height of the ceiling, which was never visible in the original, is 14 feet. The descending ramps, leading from the rear of the bridge to the helm, add to the illusion of even greater height.

In order to shoot the sets, including the bridge, in which most of the action occurs, walls are built "wild". "Wild walls" are moveable to allow for camera placement. "In order to put the camera in the right place, you have to build you sets so they can be taken apart in pieces," Zimmerman adds. "You put the camera on one side for the master, then put that wall back. Move the camera, pull another wall out and do coverage. Those are experimental matters—you either know how to do them or you learn how to do it very quickly."

Complicating matters even further is the limited amount of time available between design and execution of all aspects of the **Star Trek** production, ranging from visual effects to make-up and, of course, set design. "The norm is to get a script two weeks in advance of principal photography, and have two production meetings," explains Zimmerman. "One is a preliminary concept meeting and one, hopefully, a week or three or four days prior to the start of production. We get together in the production meeting and talk out the problems, coming up with new ideas, submit budgets and revise concepts and ideas to fit [those] budgets. We proceed as fast as we can and sometimes will start shooting a picture and not have all the elements in place for a particular scene until the night before."

"It's pretty intense," Rob Legato concurs. "I sometimes have as much as five weeks, and usually less. Ideally, you want to get the script, read it, absorb it, figure out how you're going to play out the sequences, but often in television the scripts don't come out until a couple of days before you shoot it. You have to very quickly come up with a concept and immediately have it built.. It is kind of unheard of to do the amount of work we're doing in the time we're doing it in."

According to Legato, the writers' uninhibited imaginations are providing a bevy of creative ideas which are not necessarily easily translated into reality. "They're writing it without any constraints in mind. What's a lot more interesting to do is have someone create something that is unbelievable so it has a more charged feeling on the set. The actors are acting to something that's really phenomenal as opposed to writing a dialogue scene where you have to play everything out. Instead they look at the viewscreen and see something magnificent. Well, thank you, I appreciate that."

One of **The Next Generation**'s most engaging dilemmas was retaining the look of the far more expensive feature films in its weekly **Trek** episodes. Even at an approximate budget of $1.5 million an episode, it is difficult to mirror the look of a $20 million motion picture. "We have to keep on trying," says Justman, who is encouraged by what the show has achieved so far. Wil Wheaton, who's starred in a number of motion pictures including **Stand By Me**, states, "We're not a three camera sitcom. We go on film and are transferred to video on the same setting as a feature film. It definitely feels like a feature."

Among the directors who have helmed **Trek** episodes have been Corey Allen, who directed the pilot; Richard Colla, who also directed the three hour premiere of **Battlestar: Galactica** and Rob Bowman, **Trek**'s most prolific director whose work includes "Where No One Has Gone Before" and "Too Short a Season". The cast is almost unanimous in its praise for the men behind the camera.

"We've had some good directors that have been very perceptive," Michael Dorn remarks, rubbing his bony facial appliance which transforms him from mild-mannered actor to Klingon warrior. "They know more about directing than I do and I know more about acting. If they say run out in this scene and break down and cry, I'd say he doesn't do that. The director gives you parameters and limits, but you take it and fill it up with as much color as you can."

"I think Roddenberry's gotta be pretty pumped up he turned the networks down," says Jonathan Frakes. "He had such a shitty time with them the first time."

First run syndication has notoriously been a medium for trashy two camera sitcoms and hokey revivals of failed series such as **We Got It Made** and **What's Happening**, so it came as a great surprise when Paramount announced they would bypass traditional network deals and a lucrative arrangement with the Fox Network, and syndicate the show on their own. Among the benefits that syndication holds for the show is freedom from network interference, something Gene Roddenberry was only too well acquainted with from his days of doing **Star Trek** for NBC.

"We did a scene the other day where I call Q a son of a bitch," Frakes notes, "and no one even suggested I do it another way."

Producer Robert Justman admits that while the ratings may suffer because of **Trek**'s unique broadcast method, it was a sacrifice worth taking. "My feeling is that network interference has become more objectionable. I think our ratings would be phenomenal, but we'd have lots of grief."

Brent Spiner agrees and is excited about the opportunities for creative growth syndication allows. "I certainly prefer it. I've never actually met a censor before and I'm not sure I'd like to. I think Gene himself is sort of our censor and he has a certain responsibility to the many fans of **Star Trek**, and I think he's real sensitive to that. It's not the same as having some arbiter of taste suddenly decide what is tasteful."

Almost all agree that you'd never see the Edo cavorting semi-nude on ABC. "We're already into shows dealing with certain situations you couldn't do on a network," Michael Dorn believes. "In this day and age of AIDS, networks have a responsibility. They're umbilically tired to their sponsors, but we're not under that type of gun and that's really nice...*really nice*!"

"I think they're going to try and push the limits a little," Frakes says excitedly. "It's interesting, because Roddenberry stories always have little morality plays and so to carry it into the actual production of the show makes the line very thin as to what is appropriate and what's not. I'm curious to see how it's drawn. To have it put in the creator's hands is a very powerful position and I love it. I think he likes it and I hope he handles it appropriately. One wonders if it's appropriate to call someone an S.O.B. at 6 o'clock on a Sunday night."

While the cast acknowledges that the freedom allows for a greater flexibility in addressing contemporary issues, it doesn't mean the new **Trek** will deal with them in any greater depth than its predecessor. "The old show never did it adequately," Robert Justman says, "but it did it as best it could. What the show says is that mankind will never be perfect, but the thing that makes humanity human is that we're continually attempting to reach perfection. We'll never reach it, but we keep on trying and it's the same thing with the show. We keep on trying, but we will never be able to do it as well as we would like."

"I think if we were to adequately explore these elements we wouldn't be make a television series, we'd be doing documentaries," says Patrick Stewart. "It's present always, though. There's not been an episode where there has not been a central argument dealing with a moral, psychological or social problem. I think Gene Roddenberry takes very seriously, not solemnly, what has to be done with this series and that each story is taking a view of life and has a point of view."

"A lot of the episodes have been dealing with the need for a vaccine against what has infected a planet," adds Frakes, "and that's obviously as important now. As well as terrorism and the threat of being overtaken by negative forces."

Despite the sometimes rather forceful attempts by the cast to accentuate the differences between the original **Star Trek** and the new formula, the comparison is one that plagues them like the proverbial carrot on a stick. It was particularly satisfying when William Shatner allegedly gave his tacit blessing to the endeavor. "One day our cast was eating at the commissary," explains Wil Wheaton, "and Mr.

Shatner name up and it was real tense. He said he liked it. When Captain Kirk likes the next generation, it's a big deal."

"As a friend of mine put it when I accepted the job," Stewart recalls, "how do you think it will feel playing an American icon? It did make me a little uneasy, so I'm happy that people seem to have accepted the captain as a non-American. The other thing that has pleased me is that people have written and said you are the crew of the Enterprise, and we believe in that crew. They refer to the vivid contrast between the previous captain and myself, not in a competitive way, but in that they are so different there isn't any sense of overlap."

"Some people were afraid of the new **Star Trek** because the old people wouldn't be in it," Justman states. "It was a threat to them. But I don't think that lasted very long. You form new relationships all through life. Sometimes the old relationships are the best, sometimes they're not. There's room in this work for diversity. People resist change for various reasons. It's just a natural reaction to put a show or an enterprise down out of hand, but it's not very science fictiony. The great thing about people interested in science fiction is that they have open minds. They're eager for new ideas. Otherwise, why do anything different? Let's do **Space Patrol**. It was on and people liked it."

Zimmerman agrees that while he has fond recollections of the past **Star Trek**, it does not color his approach to the present and the future design of the show. "I don't think we should be burdened with the past, only instructed by it. We give a nod backwards, but we don't look backwards for inspiration." Similarly, Rob Legato's visual effects work was not drawn from the original's lead. "People don't judge it as a TV show or as special effects. They have a warmer recollection of it, like looking at home movies. You don't look at them for the photography. It just brings back nice memories."

"We don't want people to forget the old show," asserts LeVar Burton, who plays the blind navigator Geordi LaForge in **The Next Generation**. "We're not trying to supplant in anyone's mind the affection they feel towards the old character. We just want them to give us the opportunity to be ourselves and judge us based on who we are and not compare us to something that came before us."

Brent Spiner elaborates. "It's the easiest sort of way to approach it. I think that will go away and we'll all be part of the same mold eventually."

Among almost the entire cast and crew, Gene Roddenberry is readily acknowledged as the auteur of **Star Trek**; the man who gave life to the show and oversaw its rebirth. Like Lazarus, Roddenberry supervised a resurrection of sorts which challenged him creatively and emotionally. "It's Gene's vision," Stewart says firmly. "We are caught up and embracing that vision and expanding it, but it belongs to Gene. I feel his hand everywhere and I respect it."

"This show has a style that I don't think any other show has," Frakes speculates. "That style is undefinable, but it exists and comes out of Roddenberry's scripts and thank God

he's aboard. He referred to himself the other day as the highest paid rewrite man in Hollywood. He keeps his eyes on every page of every script. It's his show, his vision and we're his players."

Roddenberry's involvement was part of what prompted LeVar Burton to accept the role as Geordi. Burton explains, "I liked the old show an awful lot, and when I heard Gene Roddenberry was also doing this one it said to me that this show was also going to be done right and with taste, dignity and integrity."

Rob Legato puts the unadulterated praise in greater perspective. "It's very interesting. He comes up with some great ideas. They're impossible, but they're great. They just write it and I wet in my pants when I look at it."

Roddenberry has directed his efforts towards refining the stories and the scripts for the series, leaving the massive logistics of keeping the show on schedule and on budget in the capable hands of producers Justman and Rick Berman, who oversee the day to day operations ranging from scheduling to color correction. Justman acknowledges that he shared Roddenberry's emotional reasons for returning to the show nearly twenty years after its cancellation. "When I left **Star Trek** in 1968, it was a disaster. It was a failure as far as the network was concerned and the industry. The only think that saved **Star Trek** two years in a row were the people who cared about it. By the time the third season rolled around, the handwriting was on the wall and Gene and I both know that it was so. I have a need to return to prove that the show did have value and was successful and could be successful again, and that you can go home again and prove to the people who doubted you that there was value there all along. That this was a worthwhile, if you'll pardon the expression, enterprise."

"One of the reasons this show didn't take the dive we all feared it would in the back of our minds in comparison to the old show," Frakes says, "is because the characters were so well thought out ahead of time."

Patrick Stewart agrees with Frakes' assessment, "One of the things that makes this show successful is the sense we have of a very distinctive group of individuals working as a cohesive whole."

Dorn laughs in agreement and adds, "This is a very happy set. I think Brent and Jonathan are two of the funniest guys I've ever worked with, and Patrick is a consummate professional with a great sense of humor."

"We have one of the best ensembles in the business," Burton proclaims. "We all respect and admire each other."

"We've always had fun. All the directors have said they've never worked on such a fun set," Marina Sirtis says in her own affable manner. "It's incredible to have actors who get along so well. It's so cliche, but we're all so happy to be here."

"I don't know how they cast this so well," reflects Frakes. "We go out to dinner after 14 hour days. They hired actors who like to act instead of hiring movie stars or models. For virtually all of us, this is the biggest job of our career and we're happy about

that. It's an ensemble and I think it's a good ensemble."

"The company takes on the personality of the leader," Justman says. "There's an old saying and it's a terribly crude expression, that the fish stinks from the head. The old show had that same feeling. We were a family. It's still the same show and it's still the same people doing it with the same personality and the same beliefs. Gene is the great bird of the galaxy and everything comes from him. That's just the way it's been and that's the way it will continue to be."

Denise Crosby, in a brief moment of introspection, reveals what appealed to her about doing **Star Trek**. "There's a lot of personal reasons why one takes a job like this, for me and my career, but also I thought it would be pretty fascinating. It's pop art to me and it's folklore. It's kind of great that way."

One other aspect that appealed to the cast was their ability to contribute input during reviews of the scripts prior to filming each episode. "We have a script meeting," reveals Michael Dorn, "and that's when we go through everything. For example, in one scene, Worf, the consummate warrior, is stalking these soldiers and when battle comes, I dodge a bayonet and trip. I said if this guy is the consummate warrior, he doesn't trip on a rock. They go you're right, and change it."

"They do take into consideration how the actors will feel about the scripts," Wil Wheaton says, "which is wonderful."

"We discuss what our feelings are and where we have problems," Spiner adds. "I think more than anything else it's a timesaver."

Patrick Stewart reveals that he would not have accepted the offer had he not been granted input into shaping the character. "For years my career has been spent on working on either classic texts with some of the very finest living writers and I have never experienced anything other than a complete openness about the creative process. If I had been denied input into what I say, I would have walked away. I have no interest in being someone else's vision and being totally locked into a third person view of the role."

While trying to downplay comparisons to the original, the new series often offers subtle reminders regarding the inspiration. "The McCoy scene was an extremely sentimental thing to do," Michael Dorn acknowledges. "I think they're just trying to be cool about it, and it's sort of a twist because we're saying we're trying to get far away from the old characters...but here you go. You could recognize we're trying to say we know where we come from, we know why we're here and we want you to know that we know also, but let us make it on our own merits."

"It was nice," concedes Brent Spiner. "It was really generous (of Deforest Kelley) to be with us then in the beginning." Frakes concurs. "There are references in the scripts where we go through old data logs and find James Kirk out of respect to the old series. It's been done in very good taste. I don't think there's any way we can or should eliminate the memory of the past."

As far as paying homage to the original inspiration, Wil Wheaton offers his own scripting suggestion: "I'd like to do 'Mirror, Mirror' again, but who am I to say? I'm only an actor, not a writer." He dismisses the comparisons to the original as groundless when made in the improper context. "If you sequelize a movie, you immediately compare it to the original. With **Alien** and **Aliens**, the only constant was LV-4, the alien and Sigourney Weaver and references were made, of course, to the mission. It was a case where the sequel was equal to or better than the original. I think that's what we're doing. We're not trying to discount the original, we are continuing the saga and trekking on."

"We're landlocked on this planet Earth," says Herman Zimmerman. "Probably not very many of us, maybe a few scientists, can appreciate what being in space is. I think the point, however, is philosophically we are talking about our everyday problems. We like stories about ourselves and our problems, and that's what we're interested in. Whether we put them in costumes of the future and generate imaginative settings, we are still dealing with good and evil, love and hate relationships and all of the basic emotions and problems that human beings are running into daily.

"That's one of the things that makes Roddenberry's view of the future so believable. It's a republican view of the future, where life can be easy. You don't have to work at something you don't like. You can find the thing that allows you to contribute and that is what you can do for a living."

Producer Robert Justman attributes the failure of science fiction on television in the past to these concerns and points out **Star Trek**'s willingness to grapple with these fundamental questions of existence on and off this planet. "Most science fiction shows were not about people, they were about special effects. They weren't about morality, or [if they were it was] in a very minimal sense. Their people were two-dimensional characters. The shows that are successful deal with the human equation: mankind, the difference between right and wrong. They deal with the things that have intrigued mankind since the dawn of time. Why do you think the Ten Commandments got written? Aesop's Fables? Man is a moral creature who is attempting to achieve a state of grace."

Ultimately, though, the old adage that the more things change, the more they stay the same is borne out. **Star Trek** for all its newfound glitz and 80s maturity, still harkens back to the essential elements which encompassed it in the 60s, and it is still wrestling with the same issues which have intrigued audiences for the last twenty years. "I think the content is much the same as it ever was," says Justman. "While our techniques may be a little slicker [and] the shows may have a better look, I think the show's content is much the same. Just because centuries have passed, we haven't dispensed of the Ten Commandments. They still work. They're simple

"I can't say I'm ever satisfied. I'm pleased. I'm never satisfied. The show could be better, but it could be a helluva lot worse. You can't turn

out a Picasso every week. Supposedly we're dealing with some kind of art. It's not possible in a collaborative effort to turn out a work of genius once a week. All we can do is attempt to win some and we'll lose others. I think no matter how bad our episodes will be, and some will be really bad, we're trying. You don't make mistakes if you don't try."

A clapboard snaps closed. A voice emanates from the bridge: "We're rolling!" The voice of Captain Picard is growing harder to discern as I leave the soundstage, some extras still mulling around outside. I pause and look back, pondering the subculture which the original **Star Trek** has generated. Thousands of conventions, fan clubs, books, buttons a Saturday morning cartoon, comics, fanzines and the like. Now, only several feet away, the same team which created it all are attempting to recapture the magic which has engaged and challenged the mind of a generation. I can't help but think of the fans who would pay untold fortunes if only to sit in the captain's chair of the Enterprise for a moment. It's quite a sight and quite a cast and crew. Unlike any other set on the Paramount lot, there's something very special going on at Stage 10.

Shaking my head, though, I can't get the sneaking recollection out of mind that has weighed on me my whole visit—the profound remark William Shatner offered on **Saturday Night Live** which is probably the most telling of all: "For God's sake, it's only a TV show!"

FIRST CHAPTER

he premiere or pilot of any television show is usually considered more significant than all other episodes of an ensuing series, for the simple reason that it lays down the groundwork for the weekly version. Here, the premise is set-up, the primary characters introduced and the audience given the opportunity to determine whether or not these are people they care about, and if their adventures are worth following week after week.

In other words, it's a crap-shoot, and depending on the roll of the dice, the series will either be a winner or a disaster.

Ironically, for all intents and purposes **Star Trek: The Next Generation** had had seventy nine live action, 22 animated and four feature film pilots, and yet the worry was still there. This **Star Trek** would be featuring an entirely new cast in a show that was similar to, yet different than, the original. Added to this was the fact that the audience for this type of show had changed since the Sixties, and one had to wonder what elements from that distinct time period would still work some two decades later. Would the current generation be as socially conscious as its predecessor?

Producer Robert Lewin, who was involved with **The Next Generation** throughout most of its first season, feels that bringing **Star Trek** back to television was a unique challenge.

"I thought starting from ground level was the only way to go," he says. "The old show was not a big hit originally, and became a big hit during the Seventies because the ideas being dealt with were advanced. While the show looks primitive now, it has a lot of content. Here, the idea was to provide the same content in a 1987 capsule; within 1987 parameters.

"We were all very, very excited about it," he adds. "The difficulty has been that the public is extremely sophisticated and the ideas that seemed new and revolutionary in the early show are no longer revolutionary. The possibility of getting new and revolutionary ideas in today's marketplace is difficult, so we struggled with that. Also, the basic idea was that the new ship had to be enormous and highly advanced, and in order to do that it needed a larger complement of command people. So we ended up with a very large crew on the bridge, and in trying to deal with the three main elements of the show—ideas, adventure and personalities—it has been a difficult combination to get exactly the best episodes possible out of each idea. Some of the shows are uneven, and some are excellent.

"Part of the problem is due to the fact that the first year of any television series is really a shake-down. I remember when I worked for Quinn Martin and he was struggling with **The Fugitive**. He said he learned how to do the show by *listening to the show*. The show told him what it had to become, and that you could not force your ideas into the show. The show

had to tell you, as long as you listened to it. That's what's going on in **Star Trek** right now. We started out with preconceptions, and some of them were very difficult to execute. It was a stimulating process, though, because we were trying to cover new ground. We discussed themes for stories and in trying to make those themes work in an adventure format, sometimes we could do it and sometimes we couldn't. We began to struggle with trying to create what we thought would be the best approach and found, as we began to work, that the show began to talk to us. 'You can't do this because (a) it's too talky and (b) the characters are not going to be developed enough.' Now we're finding that there are better ways to go. I think that more emphasis will be placed on individual relationships, which will probably be quite different than they are now on the show. But in order to deal with human beings in a framework we can understand now, we have to deal with them on a 'now' basis."

Katharyn Powers, one of the writers behind the third episode of **The Next Generation** entitled "Code of Honor," wonders if today's audience will react the same way to **Star Trek** as yesterday's did. "Remember, the show in the 60s caught on very slowly," she relates. "At first, it was your basic 20 percent hardcore science fiction audience, but then after it went into syndication it began to grow and cross over into general audience appreciation. Now, **Star Trek: The Next Generation** has so many more people who are going to be watching and the potential is that much greater. I also think that they're going to try to say something to everybody, but whether everybody will be up to listening or more up to watching the pizazz, we'll have to wait and see. Today's youth are not burning with curiosity to solve the great questions of the day. Certainly the potential is there to do the same kind of intellectual probing of mankind's position in the universe, and his responsibilities, although I don't know how many people are going to want to hear that right now."

Writer Tracy Torme, most recently Creative Consultant on the series, became involved with **The Next Generation** as a freelance writer shortly after the show's inception.

"I guess one of the most exciting things was watching the show grow from scratch," he recalls, "because when I was first involved with them, they hadn't cast anything and they really hadn't built any of the sets. It was all still in Gene Roddenberry's head. The exciting thing for me was watching it take place from the ground floor up; seeing the visualization of the characters. When I first heard about Riker, Picard and the others, I had no idea what they were going to look like or what the ship was going to look like. So I've seen some subtle changes that they've made in the characters in terms of their names, backgrounds and so on. Someday it will be interesting to look back to see where it all started from.

"One of the strengths of this series is that it is *not* a clone of the original," he elaborates. "Gene has made a real point of having this show stand on its own two feet, and he's gone out of his way to do that. He doesn't want to draw too much at all from the old show. That's a big gamble, and I respect him for taking such a chance. I think the show has been quite updated and the characters are much more for the 1980s than the 1960s."

Richard Krzemien, a writer who had penned a script for the revised **Twilight Zone** as well as the story for "The Last Outpost" episode of **The Next Generation**, believes that Roddenberry's involvement gives this show's revival a better chance at survival than that of **Twilight Zone**, which was forced to go on without the contribution of the late Rod Serling.

"Gene's being executive producer is a good aspect of the show," he enthuses. "In some ways it's evolving from the first three years of the show where...if someone else had been producing the series, there might be an entirely different tone to it. I think that Roddenberry is bringing to it a continuity that it really needs. It's sort of what wasn't there, in some ways, with **The Twilight Zone**. Obviously Rod Serling couldn't produce the series, but there was a certain vision that started that show, and a certain energy and a way of carrying that vision that Serling did best. And he found a couple of people who helped him create it. He had his hand in all the shows, and I think the vision changed drastically when Phil DeGuere took over the series. Whether it was good or bad, other people can decide that, but it wasn't the same show. I think it's a positive aspect to have Roddenberry still around to be able to produce. He pretty much sets the direction and it's like a flagship leading the cruisers behind it. That's the advantage of having some-

35

body who knows the vision of the show. He demands such high standards. How do you top yourself?

"How do you recreate values from 20 years ago, given a certain time and a certain age, and what has kept the series alive for all of this time?" Krzemien asks rhetorically. "This isn't a fluff show like most of the things on television. They were taking chances by looking at the human condition. That's what makes it so hard to write for **The Next Generation**. You can't just come up with an action shot and have somebody run across a field and get shot. You have him running across a field and they ask you *why* he's running across the field. And why is he getting shot? Why does he die? You have to answer all those questions, because if you can't, then it's wrong. If it doesn't make sense in the larger context of the story, then that's wrong too. So it takes a long time to write story ideas for the show."

Despite the enthusiasm of the staff, the question still remained: how would **Star Trek: The Next Generation** kick off its premiere season? The answer came in the form of "Encounter at Farpoint," written by Dorothy Fontana and Gene Roddenberry, which began with the galaxy class starship Enterprise on its maiden voyage to Farpoint Station, where it will pick up First Officer William Riker, Chief Medical Officer Beverly Crusher, her son Wesley, and navigator Geordi LaForge. Enroute, it is boarded by an alien being identifying itself simply as Q, who demands that Captain Jean Luc Picard turn the Enterprise around and head back in the direction from which it came. Q ac-

cuses the captain and all of mankind of being a savage, barbaric and warlike species that does not deserve to venture into the far reaches of space. Picard argues this, pointing out that man has reached maturity and that the barbarism the alien speaks of is centuries behind them. Q is absolute in his belief, refusing to listen to Picard's words, although he does admit that it will be intriguing to watch the humans futilely prove their case. This ultimately leads to Picard and company being brought to a 21st Century court, wherein Q, who has a penchant for changing costumes, is now serving as judge. Again, Picard defends his species, with Q eventually determining that the opportunity to prove himself will occur at Farpoint Station.

Once arriving there, and after new personnel transfer to the Enterprise, Commander William Riker, who now serves as Enterprise's Number One, informs Picard that anything a person could want materializes at the mere thought; that somehow thought is transferred into energy, and that thought becomes a reality. Before they can give this potential problem much attention, a much larger spacecraft arrives and begins firing energy beams at the city below, causing massive destruction.

Ultimately we learn that this alien spacecraft is, in actuality, an alien being capable of shape-changing, and that the city below—Farpoint Station, essentially—is also a living creature that is the first one's mate, who has been held as a virtual prisoner, forced by the inhabitants of that world to grant their every wish. Enterprise supplies the city-creature with enough energy to break free, while simultaneously proving mankind's tolerance and understanding of other life forms, and proving the human race has every reason to be in space. The creatures depart, as does Q, although *he* doesn't promise that they've seen the last of him.

Overall, this was a very exciting opening for **Star Trek: The Next Generation**, serving as a fine introduction of the new Enterprise crew, while presenting a fascinating antagonist. All of this is only marred by Q's condemnations of mankind as a barbaric species, which, as was stated at the outset, is rather old hat by now. Still, the two hour pilot manages to capture the best elements of the old show, while paving the way for the new.

A great deal of the credit for the premiere's success must be given to actor John de Lancie, whose abilities so successfully brought Q to life and made him a very real and tangible threat to the Enterprise crew. In fact, to make the whole thing more realistic for *him*, de Lancie created a background history for Q.

"I wanted to know who 'Q' was before we saw him here," relates de Lancie. "There may be a bunch of 'Qs', maybe fifteen of them, who operate way above the human plane. We're really talking Gods here; minds that grasp far more than the human mind is able to. Maybe he's one of the young Qs who's sitting around a table, hardly ever being asked any opinions about anything. He hears that these humans are coming into this sacred sector of the universe, and the general thought is that they pollute everything they come in contact with. I volunteer, 'Listen, I'll go out and I'll handle them.' 'You think so?' 'Yeah, sure. Can I dress up?' 'You can do anything you want, as long as you clear them; as long as we know that they're not here to disrupt.' 'Great, I'll see you later.'

"Listen," the actor elaborates, "we could sit down and talk about humans being born of Zeus, but I was trying to come up with a thing that permitted...he shoots from one to the other to the other, and then he relinquishes quite quickly. When he discovers that humans do indeed have a capacity, he relinquishes. In a wonderful way, he's got kind of an amorality to him. He's not encumbered with an opinion. He just wants to get the facts. He's not here to promote his point of view. He's out there to figure out what you're about, and as long as what you're about is okay, then everything else is okay.

"If it isn't, God help you," de Lancie laughs, adding that he took this line of thinking a bit further, trying his best to analyze exactly what sense of power "Q" held over the Enterprise crew, particularly Picard. "This is all hypothesizing, which is actor talk, but I had thought that it would be interesting that the punishment is an unravelling of Picard; a genetic unravelling of him so that he, in his attempt to make a final mark as he's getting older, or desire to leave something behind...his punishment—what he has at risk—is that I can make him disappear, not only from everyone, but from himself. I can turn him, in fact, into a non-entity, so he has something to push against. Not only does he want to be right, but he doesn't want to lose the essence of Picard and all the Picards that were before. We were just talking about the things that enrich any project. You can have the same discussions about Shakespeare and then go out and play it, but it doesn't mean you're playing of it is going to be particularly different from the person who played it before you. But if it gives you something to work on, then that's fine.

"That's the fun of a good script. A good script allows you to think. There are lots of scripts that are so bad that they have no possibility of discussion, whereas you and I can sit down over a drink and talk about all sorts of possibilities about this script because it's well written."

Ironically, long before "Q" became an element, this episode began as an outline by Dorothy Fontana entitled "Meeting at Farpoint," and it was drastically different than what ended up on the air. In that scenario, the Enterprise is sent to Farpoint Station for the same reason, but upon arrival both they and the Starseeker encounter a spacegoing gun-platform, whose inhabitants demand that the respective crews give up and transfer their people down to the planet's surface, or they will be destroyed. Starseeker is the first to act, launching photon torpedoes, but it is destroyed in retaliation. Captain Picard, realizing that this platform has more power than the Enterprise, complies, hoping that in this way he will be able to find the enemy's weakness.

Once on the surface (after leaving a skeleton crew aboard the Enterprise with members of the alien race so that the starship can remain in orbit), Picard and his people meet face-to-face with an intelligent simian race who call themselves Annoi. They want the captured humans to gather a mineral called balmine which they have a great need for, and this material will be transported to the gun platform. If they do not agree, they will be slaughtered. In the meantime, Troi is feeling someone crying out in pain, but is unable to determine who or what is the source. Riker and Macha Hernandez (who would eventually become Tasha Yar) want to launch an attack on the gun platform, which Picard agrees to.

Stowing away on one of the transport shuttles, Riker and his team manage to infiltrate the gun platform. They start searching for the engine room, which they hope to destroy, and ultimately realize that this vessel is not equipped with engines. Then, Troi is staggered by someone's emotional pain, and comes to the conclusion that they cannot destroy the platform, because it is actually a sentient being.

Essentially, we learn that the main base of the platform and the power that propels it is actually a creature, who is being used against its will. Apparently this alien being wandered into Annoi territory in weakened condition, and the simians quickly discovered that it needed balmine for nourishment. Although the mineral was available in high quantities on their home world, the Annoi thought this would be the perfect opportunity to expand their empire. They constructed a gun platform *around* the creature while it was still weak, effectively trapping it. The Annoi were willing to feed it balmine, but in small amounts designed solely to keep it alive—provided that it allow itself to be exploited as a weapon.

38

Filled with a need to survive, it agreed.

No sooner has Troi detailed this tale, than the team is captured and thrown into a holding area.

Further mental communication with the creature alerts Troi to the fact that it hates what it is being forced to do. Riker has her mentally suggest that the creature land on a deserted part of the planet where its weapons can do no harm. It agrees, does so and the force of impact smashes open the holding area so that the team can escape and, with the aid of other prisoners, overwhelm the Annoi. Picard and the others recapture the Enterprise and the creature is set free. The Annoi, it's stated, will be dealt with by the Federation, while the Enterprise, its shakedown mission a success, sets course for its next adventure.

The first thought that comes to mind upon reading "Meeting at Farpoint" is that it's considerably more action oriented than the premier episode, or subsequent series, would eventually be. Bearing in mind that when announcing **Star Trek: The Next Generation**, Gene Roddenberry had stated that the series would be much less focused on the military aspects of starship life than either the original series or feature films, one can see why they softened the adventure in later drafts. This version was truly a throwback to the 1965 second **Star Trek** pilot, "Where No Man Has Gone Before," in which the audience was given an intellectually stimulating premise wrapped up in an action/adventure format.

The Annoi, who in the first draft teleplay would be changed to the Annae and be used as the name of the people living at Farpoint Station, would have apparently been Dorothy Fontana's tribute to the popular **Planet of the Apes** film series, and one can only ponder the possibility of casting Roddy McDowall as the leader of the simian race.

In addition, we would never see another Federation starship, and Dr. Crusher's offspring was a daughter named Leslie (as opposed to son Wesley), while it's stated that Riker and Data have a long-standing friendship, whereas the actual pilot represented the first time they had met. All in all, this would have been a wonderful beginning for **The Next Generation**, but the ensuing changes would be many.

Actually, Dorothy Fontana's first draft teleplay came extremely close to the final version, detailing Enterprise's arrival at Farpoint Station to pick up personnel, and the subsequent attack of an alien vessel that approaches the planet. As in the aired episode, the other spacecraft turns out to be a sentient being, as does Farpoint Station itself, which is its mate. Naturally there are some differences, particularly in the relationships of some of the principals. But for all intents and purposes, the only addition made to the script by co-writer Gene Roddenberry was the character of Q and what he wanted.

All in all, a terrific send-off for **Star Trek**'s next generation.

SECOND CHAPTER

elevision science fiction has often suffered from budgets too small to support the necessary special effects scripts usually call for. Exceptions to this have been **V**, which was actually a miniseries, and the original **Star Trek**, which relied on powerful scripts and the acting abilities of its cast to make up for low budget FX. Due to the expense of the show, chintzy effects or not, every fourth episode or so had to be completely shipboard.

This problem raised its head again when Paramount attempted to resur-

rect the show in the mid 1970s as **Star Trek II** [see **Trek: The Lost Years**, also published by Pioneer Books, for full information], and once again with the plans for **Star Trek: The Next Generation**. Actually, this budgetary dilemma was more pronounced on the latter, because the audience would no longer sit still for anything less than the best in special effects, no matter how good the scripts and acting. Everyone involved with the new show was aware of this, and that's why it was decided early on that every other show would have to be shipboard. As fans would soon discover, that ratio increased quite a bit throughout the first and second seasons, with very few shows actually taking place off the Enterprise.

Bearing all of this in mind, Gene Roddenberry looked back at the original show's "The Naked Time," one of his favorite episodes, and one which, he felt, explored inner layers of the show's main characters. For instance, we learned the turmoil within Mr. Spock waged between his Vulcan and human halves, that Captain James T. Kirk was more in love with his ship than he could ever be with a woman, and that it was something he actually resented; Lieutenant Kevin Riley fancied himself a starship commander and Lieutenant Sulu was something of a swashbuckler at heart. This was no small feat in a one hour show, and it was something that Roddenberry wanted to use to provide insight into the new characters.

"The same basic story holds true," explains Paul Lynch, who would eventually direct the resulting episode, "The Naked Now", "in that the Enterprise contracts something from another ship and the crew begins to change. Because it's a new cast, they change accordingly. Everybody drops the way they are and lets their inhibitions come out. I'd say that 'The Naked Now' is slightly more adult and a lot more comic than the original. In that show, one of the guys [Sulu] picked up a sword and started running around with it. In this, it's much more of a character change in the way of romance and strangeness leading towards humor. Everybody in the show is affected by it in different ways, but not that dissimilar. For instance, while one person might be af-

fected by becoming more amorous in a serious way, someone else becomes amorous in a lighter sense. It's all quite subtle compared to the original, because the original episode was quite heavy-handed, like most of the original episodes were."

Roddenberry, after studying "The Naked Time," decided to do a sequel (in actuality a remake), and produced thirteen pages of a teleplay entitled "Revelations," which begins with the Enterprise receiving a distress signal from the starship Tsilkovsky; a signal interrupted by a female voice wondering if there are any "pretty boys" aboard the Enterprise. Then, a moment later, an emergency hatch is blown, effectively killing the crew of that starship. Our people beam over, and Geordi LaForge is the first to contract the disease. Once back on the Enterprise, he makes a move on Tasha which he later brushes off as a joke, but contact has been made and the disease spread. Moments later, she suggests that the two of them work out their moves together in an exercise room. In the meantime, Picard calls a meeting of his key officers to explore the situation aboard the Tsilkovsky, and that's where the Roddenberry material leaves off.

It should be pointed out that much of this script eventually made it to the air, but not without a valiant attempt by Dorothy Fontana to enact sweeping changes and give it a harder edge. Primary among the things she wanted to excise was a preoccupation with sex that these pages suggest. For instance, the initial communique from the Tsilkovsky wants to know if there are pretty boys on board the Enterprise. Then Geordi and Tasha get the

41

hots for each other, a bit disconcerting, detailing nothing about the characters except that they're a horny bunch.

Fontana's first draft teleplay had them threatened by a collapsing star, while the crew is affected in considerably different ways. Geordi remains the carrier who wishes he had normal eyesight, and bemoans the fact that he doesn't, but the first person he comes into contact with is Wesley, who, like Kevin Riley from "The Naked Time," fancies himself in command of the Enterprise. Then Tasha is determined to come up with a softer, more feminine look, and comes on to Data, but he politely refutes her advances, pointing out that he cannot help her cope with emotional needs, although he wishes he could. The disease has touched the android, causing him to try his best to behave like a "good human boy" so that he will—believing in the tale of Pinocchio, the legend he identifies with most—become human. Beverly, meanwhile, is frustrated at being the widow of a hero, because she is considered "sacred ground," and for that reason men in general are afraid to approach her as a woman. She needs a man, and Picard is the person she turns her attentions to, although the captain resists her considerable charms.

As the disease reaches Troi, she finds herself overwhelmed by the emotions of all the people around her, and proclaims that she hates never being alone in her own mind. Riker helps her and is affected, stating that he should proclaim his love for her instead of denying it. He is also fearful of traveling the route of many other starship captains, living life alone without the comfort of a woman.

Elsewhere, Picard is affected, finding himself distraught when he learns that a chunk of the exploding star may be blown out towards them, and the ship is incapable of moving due to engineering problems. Ultimately, he turns to Data, confessing that he fears for the lives of his crew and their families, and that he doesn't know if he could handle anything happening to the children on board. Ultimately, and before any serious damage can be done, Beverly Crusher comes up with a cure and everyone reverts to normal.

In short, this proposed version of "The Naked Now" is far more effective than its final form, despite it being essentially the same. The tone is far more effective than Roddenberry's previous and subsequent rewrites of it. Fontana's outline is not preoccupied with sex, instead doing exactly what the story was intended to: providing insight into the new characters.

For instance, while Geordi and Wesley would be affected in much the way they were here, Tasha became a horny bimbo. Instead, in Fontana's version she wants to be recognized as a woman instead of just a security officer; she wants to strip away her hard exterior and reveal a softer side. Beverly, while still longing for a man's companionship, points out that as the widow of a Starfleet hero, no man will come near, considering her "sacred ground." This is a wonderful character bit.

The effect the disease has on Troi is wonderful, pointing out how difficult it must be for an empath to be surrounded by the confusing minds of humans. Picard's fear of harm coming to the children fits the character perfectly, reinforcing his statement from "Encounter at Farpoint" that he is not a family man, and is uncomfortable around youngsters. Still, he is concerned for them. His fear of forfeiting their lives is a very nice touch.

Data's desire to be a real-life "boy" is a natural development for the character. He has pointed out that he would give up all of his superior abilities for the chance to be human. Riker's reaction to the disease, however, is the best. We learn that he sees himself traveling down the same path as such starship captains as James T. Kirk and Jean Luc Picard, and is afraid. Half of him wants a starship command, while the other half years for female companionship. The struggle between the two is an ongoing one, and it will undoubtedly plague him for the rest of his life.

In the final version, the character development is gone.

Director Paul Lynch, despite these faults, felt excitement about the episode and the idea of doing a new **Star Trek** television series.

"The main difference," he says, "is that the production has changed over the years. The production design of the ship and the costumes and all of that are much more futuristic 'modern' than the old series. The original show always looked like it cost a dollar ninety eight with four walls painted blue. The engine room, in the old ship, was a painting. The new engine room looks like it belongs in a spaceship in reality. It's wonderful and quite stunning."

Lynch believes that the new **Star Trek** will be every bit as successful as the original, *if* people come to it with an open mind and don't expect a retread of the first series. In addition, he's confident that the show has found its own direction, having overcome the Yin/Yang stigma of having to live up to the legend that **Star Trek** has become.

"What they're staying with," explains Lynch, "is the old morality play system of stories, and they've gotten a cast that is absolutely wonderful. Staying with the same kind of stories with a very strong cast, I would assume that the people who love the original **Star Trek** will hopefully come over to it, and if they will accept the new characters, which is the key thing, then I would think they would accept it on the same basis as they accepted the original.

"I think they're starting with a known audience for a certain kind of show," he concludes, "and they want to give them that kind of show. I think that through the first six or eight episodes you'll see **Star Trek** in a new way that's appealing. This is not Leonard Nimoy or Bill Shatner. It's a different group of people in a different situation in a future beyond that time, getting involved in compelling situations with wonderful special effects. I can't imagine what more an audience could want."

Judging by the success of **The Next Generation**'s first season, not much.

THIRD CHAPTER

"When I was started writing episodic television," explains Katharyn Powers, who, with co-writer Michael Baron penned the "Code of Honor" episode of **Star Trek: The Next Generation**, "I began on **Kung Fu**. There were many shows 10 to 14 years ago that seemed to have richer characters and more emphasis on story. Looking at the new season, I'm not impressed. I was involved in **Logan's Run, Fantastic Journey, How the West Was Won, Young Pioneers** and **Petrocelli**. These shows were very interesting to write for, and **Star Trek: The Next Generation** was an opportunity, for the first time in years, to address the bigger issues, the human issues; do interesting characters and go out of the realm of the **Falcon Crest/Dallas** soap opera mentality. I'm not that excited about writing for those shows, so the inspiration for 'Code of Honor' was to combine interesting characters with interesting problems, juxtaposed with this wonderful new cast. And even though it's a new cast, they still wanted to have the same kinds of **Star Trek** stories, the same feeling of comraderie and family. To prepare for the script, we watched many of the old episodes and the movies to immerse ourselves in 'space.'"

"There's a great deal of potential in the characters," interjects Michael Baron. "They're interesting and there are many ways they can react off of each other. It's obvious that what happened with the earlier **Star Trek** was that the characters evolved into a wonderful family. If the same magic happens with the actors in this show, I don't see why it can't be as successful. One thing we noticed in our research is that if you watch the earliest episodes in contrast to the later ones, there's a big difference in the content. It changed a great deal and that will probably happen with **Star Trek: The Next Generation** as well."

The writers became involved when they went to one of the show's many pitch meetinSgs, where they discussed several ideas.

"They liked 'Code of Honor' the best," says Baron. "It underwent many changes, but the idea was to create an alien civilization with an interesting look and a central theme to it. We based them somewhat on the Samurai culture in Japan and made parallels, which was fun to do. I've always been fascinated by Japanese culture and history."

In "Code of Honor," the Enterprise is negotiating with the people of Tellis for a very rare vaccine to a deadly disease. Beamed aboard the Enterprise is Lutan and several of his followers, who wish to make sure that the Federation are an honorable people worthy of a trade agreement. While there, Lutan becomes fascinated by Tasha Yar and then boldly kidnaps her via a transporter beam. Shortly thereafter, Picard finds himself in the position of having to ask Lutan for Tasha back, in order to "preserve honor." This is done at a ceremony wherein Lutan's mate, Yarena (who is also trying to salvage her honor), challenges Tasha to a battle to the death. This combat ultimately does occur, with Tasha proving victorious, and Yarena dying from the poison on the weapons they are using. *But* 24th Century technology brings the woman back from the dead, and in this way both Yarena and our people are able to discern Lutan's true intentions: to retain his mate's property without the woman being around to tell him what to do with it, while possibly ending up with Tasha as his new mate. If not, he'll make do with his new found riches. Of course Yarena is furious and hurt, removing Lutan as her

"First One," replacing him with someone who had been a subordinate, but was obviously deeply in love with her. Enterprise gets the needed vaccine and departs this sector of the galaxy.

As was a problem with many of the initial episodes of **The Next Generation**, "Code of Honor" bears striking similarities to the original **Star Trek**. In the "Amok Time" episode, Spock returns to Vulcan due to the Pon Farr illness that affects his people once every seven years. He gets involved in a battle to the death, and finally learns that he is the victim of a manipulating female who loves another, but has arranged this battle so that she will be able to claim his property. Although it was obvious everyone was still searching for a direction the new series could call its own, and despite the similarities, this was still a good episode.

As originally conceived by Powers and Baron, the Tellisians were a reptilian race whose philosophy mirrored that of the Samurai . The story structure is essentially the same as aired, with the added element that Lutan slowly poisons Yarena's uncle. This, coupled with the death duel between his mate and Tasha, would allow all of the man's property to fall into Lutan's hands. So desperate is he, that he orders his followers to kill the Enterprise Away Team immediately after the combat, though they are hesitant lest this result in war with the Federation. Lutan is nonetheless confident, noting that he has become allies with an enemy of Starfleet (which one can only deduce would be the Ferengi).

FOURTH CHAPTER

rom the outset of **Star Trek: The Next Generation**, Executive Producer/Creator Gene Roddenberry had made it clear that he did not want the new show to tread old ground. To this end, he created characters who were not clones of the first Enterprise crew and refused to have a Vulcan in a key position on the bridge. Initially, he even resisted the idea of utilizing the Klingons or Romulans, feeling it time to create a new threat to the Federation.

As time went on, it seemed he was as good as his word, although a Klingon (Lieutenant Worf) did serve on the bridge (as there is now peace between the Federation and the Klingon Empire) and the Romulans reappeared in the last episode of season one, "The Neutral Zone," and during the show's second year. The new "threat" became the Ferengi, an alien people driven almost completely by the love of material acquisition. The impression given by certain dialogue in "Encounter at Farpoint" is that the Ferengi are a fearsome people, and one the Federation had never actually encountered.

Richard Krzemien supplied a story entitled "The Last Outpost," which was transformed into a teleplay by producer Herbert Wright, chronicling the Federation's first contact with the Ferengi, as the Enterprise pursues one of the alien's flagships in the hopes of regaining a stolen T-9 gold extractor. They lock into orbit around a nearby planet, and both suddenly find themselves trapped...unable to escape with ship weapons and life-support systems rapidly failing. With no choice, they beam down to the planet's surface with the intention of working together to solve this mystery. But the Ferengi are quick to betray the trust, utilizing laser/energy whips to incapacitate Riker and his Away Team. The Ferengi move in for the kill, but are interrupted by a cloaked figure known as Portal, the last survivor of the Tkon Empire (which was destroyed by a super nova), who accuses all of them of being savages (shades of Q!), and decides to judge their worthiness to survive. Only Riker's knowledge and utilization of the philosophy behind **The Art of War** proves the Federation's maturity to Portal, and only Picard's compassion allows the Ferengi crew to survive.

As originally conceived, the Away Team and the Ferengi beamed down to the planet and immediately launched into an attack against each other, but were forced to work together to combat savage dog-like creatures from a crystalline chamber. Portal, known here as Dilo, confused by their actions, admitted that he had intended on destroying them as sav-

ages until they started working together for a common cause. In addition, he is later saddened to learn of the demise of his people, particularly because he is a spreader of knowledge and now there is no one to spread his accumulated knowledge. It is Riker's suggestion that this world become a library planet. "Let every nation share the information of a thousand centuries," he says. "Help us learn to lower our defenses; to surrender to wisdom and higher truth."

Frankly, if this version of "The Last Outpost" had been filmed, it would have cost upwards of three times the normal price-tag for an episode of **The Next Generation**. Overall, the episode as aired is an effective one, although the theme of accusing man of being barbaric savages already wears thin. The Ferengi are terrific and highly original villains, and their appearance here only hints at what future episodes might hold.

Richard Krzemien is philosophical about the episode, obviously grateful for the experience garnered on the show.

"Herb kept as much of my story as he could," admits the writer, "and I think most of it is there. The story evolved from a small one, when I pitched it, to six drafts later when it turned into a stepping stone to introduce the Ferengi, who are essentially the new Klingons. With that element added, it became more of the focus. The main thrust came to be how we could best develop the Ferengi.

"Admittedly," he continues, "it was hard to come up with a payoff for that episode. We had to introduce these people with this major problem, and then you had to come up with an ending that made it worthy of the set-up of the beginning. That was hard right from the start. I think the first half of the show is really dramatic. There's a lot of things happening, and all of those things have to be tied up at the end. You could start off developing a great show, but if you can't tie it up, it just doesn't work."

He notes the many changes between original concept and final script. "In the script they're confronting the Portal," Krzemien explains, "who is something of a cloaked creature. He represents the entrance to the Tkon Empire. Originally that Portal was a small guy named Dilo, who was the caretaker of this planet, and he was meant to be a light, upbeat kind of character who got caught asleep when his entire group of planets died. This is where the successive drafts came in. The concept of that still exists, but it's how Dilo is embodied that changed. That was essentially the main change from my story. That was in the fourth and fifth acts. The first three are basically the same, with the ship getting caught around the planet and getting confused by the fact that they think the Ferengi are doing it, but in fact the planet's really got both of them. Again, it was how do you pay that off on sort of a grand scale? Gene Roddenberry likes to have galactic ideas and themes dealt with. Having a noble civilization die and yet having its values carried on by its gatekeeper was an interesting concept to him."

FIFTH CHAPTER

One of the finest episodes of **The Next Generation**'s initial season was "Where None Have Gone Before," written by Diane Duane and Michael Reaves. Their story was merely the fourth presented, and yet it would take over a dozen episodes for any other to even come close.

Many writers who penned stories for the first season complained vehemently about the rewrites done to their material by executive producer Gene Roddenberry and other members of the show's staff, and often times their anger was justified. And yet, despite the fact that Duane and Reaves were not that pleased with the script's final direction, one must say in Roddenberry's defense that he did a wonderful job on the rewrite. This is not a criticism of the original outline, treat-ments or scripts by Duane and Reaves, for theirs is just as good. Frankly, this situation proves similar to the one that occurred on the original series with "City on the Edge of Forever." Harlan Ellison had written the treatment and script for that episode, and Roddenberry did an uncredited rewrite. The resulting episode is considered by many to be **Star Trek**'s finest hour, winning the Hugo Award. Ellison was nonetheless angry about the rewrite and pointed out that his script was infinitely better than what they ended up with. Supporting his claim that the script was highly imaginative is that his original teleplay also won the Hugo Award. This, as well as "Where None Have Gone Before," serves as ample proof that the same idea can go in two different directions, but end up with equally workable results.

"We really lucked out," admits Reaves. "It was our concept and everything, but we were massively rewritten. I will agree that it was the best episode [at that time]. Yes, they had an all-powerful alien, but at least he was not a cranky child. One of the things we liked about the show as aired, is that there was some honest emotion involved, although not nearly as much as we had. I've only seen a few episodes of the show, but so far it seems very one-note to me. At least this alien had some problems; some things he wanted to accomplish that were viable within the **Star Trek** universe. Also, one thing they did keep from our story is that this was a problem that was not solved by slowing something up, which I kind of liked. Production-wise it was wonderful, and the acting was all very good. It came together much better on the screen than we thought it would when we read the script. We were lucky, because it was out of our hands."

As aired, "Where None Have Gone Before" deals with a Federation scientist named Kosinksi, and his assistant known simply as the Traveler, who boards the Enterprise with a formula that will considerably enhance the ship's warp speed capability. Plans to utilize his program are put into effect, but a terrible mishap occurs and the Enterprise finds itself hundreds of thousands of lightyears away from where it should be. Another attempt is made, and the ship is pushed even further away, achieving a distance that no one had gone before, and where no one would soon ever be. At this location, reality starts to break down, and the crew begins experiencing various hallucinations. For instance, Worf finds a Klingon targ (essentially a wild pig) on the bridge, Tasha momentarily finds herself back on the hell-hole of a world she was found on, Picard encounters his long-dead mother, and other crewmembers find themselves living out either fantasies or nightmares. They must, it rapidly becomes apparent, find a way home before they lose all sense of what is real and what is not.

In the meantime, Wesley has discovered that the Traveler is the one behind the enhancement of the warp engines, and the one inadvertently responsible for their current situation. In the boy, he, in turn, senses a genius—another Beethovan or Einstein—who must be given the opportunity to develop his abilities naturally. Picard, who has taken a momentary break from their predicament to listen to these words, accepts the Traveler's proclamations, and by episode's end, after everything has been restored to the way it should be, makes the youth an acting ensign.

As stated earlier, "Where None Have Gone Before" is, quite simply, spectacular, with wonderful special effects, a cast handling themselves masterfully and Rob Bowman's direction of the superb script right on the money. There is, however, one complaint. "The Naked Now," not to mention numerous episodes of the old show, already explored the idea of hidden thoughts coming to the surface, and this seems only a variation of the theme. Such repetition is slightly disconcerting, but acceptable in this case.

Also interesting to note is that this is the first time Wesley Crusher is treated with the respect he deserves, and it's good to see this positive direction given to the character. In fact, Duane and Reaves had intended this respect for his mind to be apparent in this story, even without the presence of the Traveler. In their outline, Kosinski is amazed that Riker has gone to Wesley for an opinion, and acted on it. Riker's response is that if he didn't value the boy's opinion, he wouldn't have asked for it. In addition, once that opinion was given, why wouldn't he accept it?

Even earlier than this, in the "Code of Honor" outline by Katharyn Powers and Michael Baron, the writers noted that during a key crisis, "Picard's wisdom and experience are evident in the way he supports the boy—and the calm he imparts to keep the youngster intensely focused without becoming unnerved." This is a much better approach than having the bridge crew tell the boy to shut up every time he makes a suggestion, particularly after these suggestions continually save the ship.

As initially conceived, Kosinski himself was responsible for the warp speed enhancement, as well as the accident that ensued. His character was also much more fully developed, with his balancing a career with the raising of a son, who wishes that his father had more time for him. The crew of the Enterprise, conversely, hold the man's accomplishments in awe, believing that, if successful, they will be able to further man's exploration of the galaxy. Picard in particular is impressed, believing the resulting warp capability may enable them to discern whether the universe was created by a divine force.

As in the aired version, there are two leaps via the new technology, and the Enterprise finds itself in a far distant area of space where reality starts to break down, though to a much more dramatic degree. Riker finds a welt on his arm from a bite he had once gotten from an animal, Picard finds the lifeless body of Jack Crusher on the bridge, but it disappears soon thereafter; Beverly is on the ruined deck of the Stargazer, and standing in front of her is Captain Picard, holding Jack Crusher's body outstretched in his arms.

The only solution to these visions is for the ship to get back to its own galaxy, and ultimately the Enterprise materializes within a monoblockk; a cosmic egg, which is supposed to be similar to the one which exploded and created our universe. Because ship engines have been weakened from the journey, the crew attempts to absorb energy from the monoblock to recharge them. Kosinski believes that since the monoblock exists outside normal time and space, the ensuing explosion might "kick" them back into their own universe. The attempt is made, and the Enterprise materializes *exactly* where it should be.

It is Picard's feeling that perhaps they had help; that perhaps in that moment of creation, something realized they weren't supposed to be there, and sent them home. Riker counters by musing that perhaps they themselves were the creators. There is no response to that statement, although Data informs them that the Enterprise has been away for exactly six days. Not missing the irony of that, or the universe left behind, Picard suggests that they take the seventh day off.

"There was talk at the time, very briefly, that this would be the pilot episode," says Michael Reaves, "because they needed something out-reaching. Instead, it's *just* television. The ironic thing is that Gene Roddenberry likes stories where the Enterprise meets God. We went one better. We gave him a story where the Enterprise *becomes* God! The upshot of our outline was that they wind up in an unexploded monoblock, and in order to get back to their own space and time, they have to imbalance the monoblockk, causing it to explode and a new universe to begin. The irony is that when they're doing a little low budget science fiction show, no one pays any attention. When they're pouring this kind of money into it, everybody has to commit. That's what upsets me, because here was an opportunity that I feel was missed."

As stated previously, both the Duane/Reaves outline and script and the version as aired, "Where None Have Gone Before" is *good* **Star Trek**, and no higher compliment need be paid.

SIXTH CHAPTER

In "Lonely Among Us," next up on **The Next Generation** trail, the Enterprise is escorting diplomats representing the reptilian Selay race, and the "furry" Anticans, who hate each other with tangible venom. A peace conference at Parliament may be the only way to stop them from going to war.

Meanwhile, the Enterprise passes through what seems to be a harmless energy cloud, and accidentally picks up a sentient being which enters the vessel through ship circuitry. Then, it passes from a console into Lieutenant Worf, from him to Doctor Crusher and then to Captain Picard. As one with the captain, they realize that they have much in common, and as one they beam themselves back into the heart of the energy cloud, where

they will explore the universe together. But something goes wrong, and Picard is suddenly "stranded" out there. Utilizing the transporter memory circuits, Riker and Data are able to lock onto the captain's energy pattern, and beam him back aboard. And, so, everyone lives happily ever after, with the exception, perhaps, of the Selay ambassador, who has been killed and eaten by the Anticans.

All in all, "Lonely Among Us" is a fairly effective episode with an original premise. If nothing else, it was proof that **Star Trek: The Next Generation** was finally beginning to establish its own identity.

Also, the motivation for the alien taking over the bodies of crewmembers, culminating with Captain Picard, is a wonderful one: curiosity. Essentially, it wants to know what makes us tick —and that's a refreshing change from aliens who want to use human hosts to take over the galaxy or who condemn us as savages.

Important to note is that the idea of using the Enterprise to transport ambassadors from warring planets to a peace conference was quite similar to the original show's "Journey to Babel." This was done on purpose, as explained by the scriptwriter for both, Dorothy Fontana.

"In 'Lonely Among Us' I pulled from myself," she admits, while agreeing that elements from old shows appeared in many of the early episodes, "in that the mission was to transport these diplomats from here to there. The flow, however, was entirely different. Besides, they were a subplot to be in point a fun kind of thing, as opposed to serious 'drama,' like in 'Babel.' So what I did was pull from myself and switch it around. I feel there's a difference between the two. There's a definite delineation and separation here, both in intent and content."

The episode began as a treatment by Michael Halperin, which begins with Enterprise dilithium crystals suffering a breakdown. The ship has to go to Capella V for repairs, and the journey will take some 72 hours. Enroute, they encounter a flickering energy tree-like structure (a variation of this idea would eventually be utilized in the episode "Datalore"). Worf suggests that they fire a photon torpedo into the cloud, so that sensors can take readings of the energy levels given off. This last point is moot, as ship sensors would be able to gather this information without the need for detonating a torpedo within the cloud. This does, however, come into play (rather contrived) when Geordi and a "grunt" are in the midst of repairing the tractor beam emitter via shuttle-craft, when a particle of energy strikes the grunt. He goes crazy, doing his best to fight off Geordi, who attempts to help him.

Once the duo is back on board the Enterprise, Tasha escorts the grunt to sickbay, and an electrical charge passes between them. She is filled with unexplained anger for a short time, but this passes as the alien entity leaves her body. We are told, however, that both she and the grunt remain under its "distant" control, which is an interesting variation from the aired version. There, as detailed above, the Enterprise picks up this life form by passing through the energy cloud, and the "possession" of the crew only occurs to one person at a time.

The entity eventually goes from Tasha to Beverly, and from her to Wesley, who in turn transfers it to Data. On the bridge, it moves on to Worf. Troi eventually realizes that someone or something has been taking over various members of the crew. Later, she confides to Riker that in many people she is sensing *two* personalities, as though something is sharing their minds. However, it's only a short matter of time before Riker is possessed as well. Picard confronts him, and the commander goes into a trance, with the alien speaking through his mouth. We learn that it is desperate to survive, and means no harm to human beings. Unfortunately, it was taken aboard the ship by accident, as a result of the exploding photon torpedo. If it is not returned to its own galaxy, it will die. This is made even worse when they discover that if it dies, so will the sum total of eons of evolved intelligence. According to the treatment, "The Enterprise will have destroyed a higher-level inner universe."

Picard's real dilemma is that the ship is so close to Capella V, and will not have enough power left to make the journey back again. He then decides to use the "slingshot effect" (last utilized in **Star Trek IV: The Voyage Home** as a method of time travel) to return the ship to Capella V to an earlier time with minimal fuel loss. The momentum of their trajectory will provide enough "push" to the alien to send it back to the cloud. The entity explains that it will share its knowledge of humans with the rest of the cloud, and suggests that perhaps they will one day meet again. The slingshot effect is completed, the alien is sent home and the Enterprise arrives at Capella V.

After Michael Halperin handed in this story, he was cut off and the treatment was put on the shelf. When the show ran into a script crunch during its first season, Dorothy Fontana suggested ways to save the story, and hence went about adding the previously discussed elements. The final result is an enjoyable hybrid of both writers' efforts, although by having Picard becoming one with the alien and transporting into the cloud in the pursuit of greater adventure, Fontana added a highly enjoyable humanistic element to what could have been merely another **Invasion of the Body Snatchers**.

SEVENTH CHAPTER

"'Justice' is about the human answer to what you do when violence in the streets becomes rampant," explains writer John D.F. Black, who had served as the original **Star Trek**'s first story editor, authored "The Naked Time" and was one of the first people invited aboard **The Next Generation**. "What do you do if you're a colony? What do you do, and how would it look to somebody else when you have responded in the only way you can?

"It has to do with justice,' he adds. "For everybody, and how you deal with terrorism and anarchy. How do you stop it? And once you've stopped it, what happens next? Let's say that what we do is kill everybody who is a terrorist or suspected of being a terrorist. Now the people who have killed everybody, what do they do? We're talking about a society dealing with some aspect of itself. And this society is made of of Earth people who went out there to set up their own democratic society. It's what corrupted the Greek democracy."

John D.F. Black's version of "Justice" differed drastically from the aired episode. As aired, the Enterprise, after depositing an Earth colony, proceeds to the planet Edo, which seems to be ideal for shore leave. An Away Team, including Wesley Crusher (who represents the young people aboard the ship), beams down and meets with the head council of this world, who welcome them with open arms. What we rapidly learn is that this world is something of a paradise, with total peace and complete openness about emotions and sexuality. There is no crime due to a process by which certain areas at certain times are zones in which *any* crime, no matter how big or how small, is punishable by instant execution. Unfortunately, Wesley Crusher steps on some flowers after inadvertently committing the crime of walking on the grass. Now, he is to be terminated, although a certain delay has been granted because he is alien to this world.

Picard's problem stems from the Prime Directive, which forbids him from interfering with the natural progression of a planet. Still, how can he allow Wesley to die for such a nonsensical crime? To make matters worse, an alien muckity-muck floating in space is interfering with ship functions, while demanding that the Enterprise leave this area of space, taking all humans with it.

The episode as described really doesn't work for a couple of reasons. First, once again we are seeing this show's preoccupation with sex, which is fine when it's done for a reason, but annoying when it seems as gratuitous as it does here. Secondly, the idea of using a booming alien voice—essentially God—to manipulate the plot has been done time and time again on both the old show and the new. Here it seems to be a tired retread of what's come before.

In Black's original version, the Enterprise has been ordered to investigate the planet Llarof, an experimental Earth colony practicing the pure democracy of the ancient Greek principle of "demos." It's been 80 years since the last contact between the Federation and the colony. An Away Team beams down, and is immediately told by a police officer that they should walk on the right as the law demands, and that they should consider themselves lucky that this isn't "the day." Eventually they decide to contact the planet's government, and learn that 80 years earlier terrorism had run rampant on this world, but by instituting their system of government, they have successfully been able to put a halt to it. Our people are told that at a randomly selected time

each day, computers are triggered which locate a quadrant for a specific amount of time that serves as a place where all crimes are punishable by death. These crimes can include, as an example, speeding, and the passengers in the car would be sentenced as co-conspirators and put to death as well.

One of the council members, Trebor, is so proud of this planet, that he suggests the Enterprise use it for shore leave. Tasha is horrified, stating that they will not allow children to be murdered. Trebor tells them not to worry, that the Capital area will not be included in the computer's choosing, as it never is.

Thus far, we've seen an interesting building of a mystery. In addition, there is something truly frightening about the leader of a planet who can speak so casually of a system in which those guilty of, or thought guilty of, crimes are exterminated in a way that is similar to our stepping on a blade of grass.

The Away Team returns to the Enterprise, where they discuss the situation on the planet and the viability of shore leave. Aspect Experts voice concern over Llarof's prison system, as each building has been constructed to hold somewhere between twelve and nineteen thousand people, and yet there are only twelve in each. Picard thinks Riker should talk to Trebor about this.

In the meantime, shore leave parties do beam down, and the children— under the supervision of Enterprise security officers—are apparently having a great time. Things turn tragic, however, when two children are play fighting, accidentally fall down a slope and come to a halt between local police chasing criminals. One of the cops, Siwel, raises his weapon. Enterprise security officer Tenson pleads that they are from the starship and thereby immune, but the cop nonetheless pulls the trigger and kills Tenson. The other officer, Oitap, screams to the shooter that those people were off-limits, and with that reluctantly kills the offending officer, as the law dictates.

In the aired episode, no one from the Enterprise was actually killed.

The earlier draft gives a much more tangible sense of the justice system on Llarof. It's one thing to talk about exterminating people for the barest of infractions, but quite another to actually see the process in action. Also, the killing of Siwel by Oitap shows the seriousness by which this system of justice is followed.

Elsewhere, Riker and Picard are discussing the prison situation with Trebor. He is told the prisoners are exterminated on their "day," and the twelve people in each are actually guards. Then, news of Tenson's death starts spreading, and the Enterprise personnel immediately move to beam back aboard the starship. One man, Reneg, sensing what the Federation stands for, fills Riker in on some of the planet's history, emphasizing that doctors, scientists and the governing body were considered the elite class and were spared from possible executions. The system of elections established 80 years earlier was abolished. Immunity began to be handed down from generation to generation as though a royal inheritance. The people became fearful, and that fear be-

gan to rule their lives. No one had the nerve to challenge the government or to demand a return of the elections. Reneg adds that nearly every family has lost at least one member under this system, and that in itself is enough to cause a revolution. Both Picard and Riker point out that they cannot interfere, and that even listening or counseling him could be seen as an act of interference.

Later, the Aspect Experts state that there is combat going on in all parts of the planet, with the exception of the government area. Picard uses Federation doctrines to his advantage, pointing out that there is a rule where a starship captain can make sure that fair elections are being held where the attempt is made. Therefore, it can be reasoned that Reneg is running for office, so to this end Riker and Tasha beam down as "observers."

With barely any assistance from the Away Team, Reneg is able to launch his planned revolution, and the election process is returned to the planet.

This version of "Justice," for the most part, would have worked as an effective episode of **The Next Generation**. The theme, as previously discussed, is fascinating, and the idea of immune status being handed down from generation to generation is simply wonderful. However, it's not surprising, considering Gene Roddenberry's determination to stay as far away from the original show as possible, the ending was dropped. Riker and his Away Team serving as "observers" of the situation, who actually play a part—no matter how small—in the revolution, is right out of the old show. Captain Kirk often reinterpreted the Prime Directive to fit his way of thinking, a perfect example of which occurred in "A Taste of Armageddon." The primary difference between Black's first and second drafts is that the Enterprise personnel play a much larger role in what happens (with Wesley being one of the children who slide down the slope). It is Reneg's hope that Picard's intervention to save the children will result in a breakdown of the justice system on this world, thus allowing the people to revolt. All of this eventually leads to a trial, wherein the children of the Enterprise are set free thanks to Riker's information concerning Reneg's motives. Reneg, in turn, is executed in front of everyone for treason. All starship personnel return to their vessel, and the Enterprise breaks orbit.

On the bridge, Riker tells Picard that Reneg was probably right in regards to this system of justice, but the captain emphasizes that is not their place to judge; perhaps the people would want to leave things exactly the way they are.

"Perhaps they'd rather risk being legally executed for dropping a piece of paper on the sidewalk," Picard muses, "to live without fear of being raped or robbed or murdered in their sleep. In any case, they have a right to choose their own system of justice."

This version works far better than the first draft does, and it ends on a somewhat downbeat note, which the original **Star Trek** was able to pull off wonderfully. The courtroom scene serves as a better setting for the conclusion of the episode than an action-filled revolution would have. The death of Reneg, if filmed, would have been shocking to the audience. This was terrific drama, and the only bit of business missing is Riker's guilt for having the man confess the truth and then being killed for it. One would imagine that the commander would at least feel pity towards the other man.

"I'd been trying to do this story for years and years," explains John D.F. Black. "It's been in my mind and there's been nowhere to hook it. It would have to be a movie or something like **Star Trek**."

Unfortunately, Black would not take this story any further. As longtime **Star Trek** fans know, he left his story editing position after thirteen episodes because Gene Roddenberry insisted on rewriting every script. Feeling his position was being compromised, he left the series.

"Gene Roddenberry is Gene Roddenberry again," he explains, cryptically. "He didn't sound any different today talking to me than he sounded when I was sitting with him on the old **Star Trek**. The same things are on the line. G.R. is still G.R., as he was. He exposes himself as a human being to writers at the same level now as he did before. His own human situation, his history...everything. He's no different. He's suddenly Albert Einstein's Theory of Relativity in place."

Writer Worley Thorne took on the next two drafts of "Justice," and between his work and that of Gene Roddenberry, they crafted the episode as aired, with an incredible preoccupation with the sex lives of the people of Edo, and the intervention of a God-like being. Unfortunately, something was lost in the transition.

EIGHTH CHAPTER

The Ferengi reared their ugly little heads again in "The Battle," which was scripted by producer Herbert Wright from a treatment by the late Larry Forrester.

In this story, Damon Bok, a Ferengi commander, delivers to Captain Picard the remains of his first vessel, the Stargazer. It had engaged in battle with a Ferengi vessel years earlier, the result being that the other ship was destroyed while Picard and his crew were forced to abandon the Stargazer. Picard isn't sure what to make of this, but he accepts the gift, utilizing tractor beams to tow it alongside the Enterprise. Unbeknownst to him, Bok has a hidden agenda, which includes a pair of mind control devices. Ultimately, they cause Picard to go from having severe migraine headaches to being possessed by full-blown hallucinations of his time aboard the Stargazer, reliving the final battle in his mind. Finally, the captain breaks off the tractor beam, transports over to the Stargazer and prepares to take on the Enterprise, which he believes to be the Ferengi vessel from years ago.

We learn that Bok's only son was killed in that battle so long ago, and that he has spent his entire life preparing this revenge. The only hope comes from the unlikely source of the Ferengi first officer, who tells Riker that Bok has been arrested for participating in unprofitable business exercises. He also details the operation of the mind control devices, so that Riker can convince Picard to destroy the one on the Stargazer which is controlling his mind.

As aired, "The Battle" is a delightful episode of the series, and one which is highly original as well. Director Rob Bowman manages quite a bit of suspense, the Wright/Forrester story is excellent, and Patrick Stewart is superb as Picard, particularly during moments when he is interacting with the "ghosts" of his former crew aboard the Stargazer. Considering that he acted alone, and the other images were superimposed later, this was quite an acting feat.

Many stories change between first draft outline and final script, others remain virtually intact. The latter is the case with "The Battle," as the storyline follows the treatment quite closely, albeit in expanded form, and in turn the aired episode is similar to Herb Wright's first draft teleplay. Many early drafts of **Next Generation** teleplays focus more on character interaction than do the shows themselves. This was no exception, particularly where Picard and Beverly Crusher are concerned. There are some really nice moments when they begin to explore their feelings for each other, as well as their shared past, as her late husband, Jack Crusher, had served under Picard on the Stargazer. In fact the man's death, and Picard bringing his body home to Beverly and Wesley, was supposed to be a central aspect of their relationship. This was dealt with slightly in the premiere episode, "Encounter at Farpoint," and then only touched upon peripherally since. Ironically, an early draft of the fourth episode, "Where None Have Gone Before," dealt with this issue in an illusionary and powerful sense, but the sequence never made it to the screen. Later, in

"Arsenal of Freedom," they are trapped in a cavern, struggling to stay alive. An early draft of that episode showed their feelings for each other, but that too was ultimately dropped. Now that Gates McFadden has been removed from the show, we'll never see this element developed further.

In his draft, Forrester felt it necessary to devote a significant amount of story time to the Ferengi, going aboard their vessel and providing conversations between them. This could have provided insight into this race, in some ways mirroring relationships on board the Enterprise, and elevated them above the role of stock villains. Played for laughs after being presented as an awesome threat to the Federation, the Ferengi never became very popular . Providing a counter-balance between them and "us," Forrester was establishing a situation much like the original series episode "Balance of Terror," which introduced the Romulans.

The Ferengi have not been seen since this episode.

NINTH CHAPTER

*I*f there was one guest star of **The Next Generation** who leaped off of the television screen, it had to be John de Lancie, who portrayed the enigmatic Q in "Encounter at Farpoint." So popular was he, that he made his second appearance in "Hide and Q."

"Q can be a little 'more' than he was before," explains de Lancie of his character's return. "When he's playful, he's more playful. When he's angry, he's more angry. He's a little more relaxed. The ways in which he tries to get his way are more varied, all the way from the beginning where he's being very much the joker and bombastic, then going from being kind of sly and full of himself and then I do a scene where it's very straight. It's almost like two guys

having a cigarette, where one is saying to the other guy, 'God, I don't know how much I can really appeal to you to think this through.' It just goes back and forth and back and forth, and then his deciding to 'become' a priest. Having so much fun, and the constant baiting of Picard."

Besides being pleased with the chance to return as Q, de Lancie feels the entire production had improved in-between his episodes.

"I was there the day after the pilot aired and everybody was kind of flushed with the general feeling of having done a good job," the actor recalls. "I think the second show was very good. So they all had a sense that they were on the right track. It's fun. You have a group that works hard and is successful, and is gaining in success as they begin to see what they have. Everybody is a lot more open. The director of 'Hide and Q', Cliff Bole, is someone to whom I can say, 'Let me try it this way.' Everybody's much more relaxed. When you come onto a set where things are not going well, usually the control freaks stop down and it's dense. But it's just the opposite on that show.

"The ship kind of has headway now, and it will gain steam, I believe, as people become more and more confident about what it is that they're doing. But I think that this is light years ahead of most of the crap you see on television. And you have to understand that it's still the same medium, isn't it? And the same restrictions, the same time allotment, and yet they're really beginning to pull things off.

"It's almost like a play," he continues. "I also thought it was really clear and interesting that Q would come back after all this farting around with these guys. He'd come back and say, 'Look, there's something you have that I need.' It almost made me think about reading **The Foundation Trilogy** (in which Harry Seldon develops a system of forecasting the future). The enormous amount of time that they talk about, and the fact that Q is actually capable of seeing that far in advance, and is capable of coming to realize that the human race, if it continues at this sort of intellectual pace, will *overtake* the Q."

As de Lancie has explained it, Q returns to the Enterprise, fully cognizant (as a result of their encounter at Farpoint Station) that mankind is indeed destined for greatness. To help understand the human equation a lit-

tle better, he decides to bestow upon Riker the power of the Q so that the commander and he can become as one. This forces Riker to come to grips with his newfound power, while somehow resisting the temptation to use it in ways that would alter destiny. We gradually witness the corruption by absolute power, a theme slightly reminiscent of the second **Star Trek** pilot, "Where No Man Has Gone Before." But Riker is forced to reality by his fellow crewmembers who each, one by one, reject his offer to make their dreams come true. Again Q fails and is zapped away by his fellow Qs at the end of the episode.

In the original treatment of this story, Q makes the crew play out these bizarre games because, as Picard notes, the alien is like a child with no idea how to make friends, so he plays games with them. Picard assumes Q has a favor to ask, but doesn't know how to do so. The captain is right. We learn there are only three Qs, and the planet they reside on is dying, so they need to relocate. Naturally, Picard reasons, the Q have the power to move themselves, but, as the alien explains it, there are a little over a hundred thousand inhabitants on their world, and they don't know where to go. They need a planet which will supply the same kind of isolation they have now. Picard says he will have to discuss this problem with Starfleet.

While the early portion of the first draft treatment by Maurice Hurley follows the aired version, the ending falls apart. Besides the fact that there really is no conclusion, the idea that Q needs the Enterprise's help to move his people is a bit hard to believe. With everything we've seen this alien do, there's no way you could convince anyone that he and the others like him couldn't replenish their world. The final script, written by Gene Roddenberry and C.J. Holland, is far more effective, and his purpose is much more intriguing. In fact, one cast member compared the story to the last temptation of Christ, and that may not be too far from the truth, as Riker is torn between remaining human and something akin to being a God.

"Hide and Q" leaves the viewer wondering whether this unique alien will return. During the second season he would show up again in "Q Who?", with rumors of yet another return set for the third year. de Lancie has his own feelings about Q's return, and where he would like the character to go.

"I take 'em as they come," he smiles. "I'd like to play Q five or six more times. Whether I can or not is another thing, but I think to leave a legacy of Q episodes out there would please me. It's a good group, they've been kind to me and it's fun. As far as the direction, I have no idea. I keep thinking of Q in terms of what it would be like to meet the others Qs. We had a wonderful thought—one of the makeup guys and I—that one day if you would ever pull away Qs face, it would reveal the universe. Or maybe the next time Q comes back, he's lost all that playfulness and he's just f—ing angry. I thought of one story where he goes back and is going to get Picard...I mean *truly* get him. The way that he's going to get him is to go back in time and screw up his mother and father. You could do any-thing you want, but that's provided they want to use Q again, and I'm not in the decision-making process other than being available or not being available.

"If I were writing this," de Lancie elaborates, "I would love to explore the nature of the Q. Where is the Q continuum and what is it? I think that would be kind of like going back to Krypton. It would be kind of fun to go there and say, 'My God, this is where they all live!' These are just actor's thoughts, but another thing we thought of it is what would happen if Q was on five in a row and actually became a member of the Enterprise. Then he has to deal with whatever that means, and dealing with humans on a constant basis would keep him in therapy."

TENTH CHAPTER

One of the most confusing aspects of **Star Trek: The Next Generation** has been the relationship between Riker and Troi. In "Encounter at Farpoint." The show quickly establishes that they have something of a shared past, and signs indicate the relationship will develop as the series goes on. Ironically, these characters strike an interesting similarity to the romance between Commander Decker and Lieutenant Ilia in **Star Trek: The Motion Picture,** wherein those two people came together, we learned that they had once been involved, and the film culminated with their joining Vejur to become one being; a hybrid of man and machine.

In **The Next Generation,** there has been an occasional hint towards con-

tinuing the romance between Riker and Troi, but it has more often been forgotten. The "Haven" episode, however, dealt somewhat with Riker's reaction to Deanna Troi having to undergo a pre-arranged wedding ceremony, which will take place aboard the Enterprise between her and her pre-determined mate, Wyatt. In fact, writer Tracy Torme presents a wonderful moment where Deanna forces Riker to acknowledge that a starship is his true love, and that the chance of someday captaining a vessel is too great a temptation for him.

As though Deanna's situation is not tough enough, there are two additional problems. First, her mother, Laxana Troi, comes aboard, and she creates complete chaos by insulting virtually the entire crew via her Betazoid telepathic abilities and a complete devotion to honesty (coupled with a healthy ego). Then a plague ship approaches a paradisiacal world known as Haven, whose inhabitants do not want potential death to infect their home. Picard is must keep the dying people away from Haven, without destroying them in the process. In addition, Wyatt, who has presumed he has been telepathically linked with Troi for all these years, discovers the woman whose features he has painted and sculpted does not resemble the counsellor. Ultimately he discovers this woman aboard the plague ship. Destiny demands the couple be united, and to this end Wyatt has himself beamed over.

While not entirely successful, "Haven," at the very least, presents an original story and develops Troi and her relationship with Riker.

The original version of this story, entitled "A Love Beyond Time and Space," provided many of the story beats, but was unusable, as the characters lacked consistency, and there were too many holes in the plot. Writer Tracy Torme breathed new life into the story.

"'Love Beyond Time and Space' was written by a writer who I really don't think understood science fiction," Torme points out. "When they offered it to me, I had mixed emotions. The bad was that I couldn't even get through the outline that had been written, and the good was that I thought it was *so* unusable that anything I did would be an improvement. It was a no-lose situation for me in a way, so I told them the story would only work as a comedy. I wanted to do a broad comedy about these two families who couldn't really stand

each other, but wanted to go through with the wedding.

"My version was more caustic and the comedy had a sharper edge to it," he says, comparing the script to the aired episode. "'Haven' was rewritten maybe 20 or 30 percent, and most of the comedy was softened and taken out of the original piece, so the net result was that I didn't particularly like it when it first aired, and it's still one of my least favorite shows that I've been involved with, but for some reason it's popular among fans. I'm grateful for that. Maybe when I see it again in repeats down the road, I'll feel better about it."

ELEVENTH CHAPTER

Time travel has often played an integral role in the genesis of **Star Trek**, providing some of its best stories, such as Harlan Ellison's "City on the Edge of Forever" and the feature film, **Star Trek IV: The Voyage Home**. While the premise has not been used yet in **The Next Generation**, the next best thing has; the ship's holodeck allows a user to recreate any time period on any planet stored in the Enterprise computer memory banks.

This device works to its best advantage in Tracy Torme's second effort for the show, "The Big Goodbye." The holodeck recreates the fictional world of 1940s detective Dixon Hill. Then when the computer malfunctions, it traps Captain Picard and several other crewmembers in very real

danger in the artificial reality. This created an interesting problem for the episode's director, Joseph Scanlan. He had to combine the world of the Enterprise with the fictional past of Dixon Hill, while still sustaining the reality for the audience.

"Combining the past with the future world was a little difficult, and that is indeed what we had to do," explains Scanlan. "The holodeck, in my opinion, was never totally clear as to its function to the audience, and it's the first time that people, in effect, got trapped in it because of a malfunction of the equipment. They're trapped in the past, and yet it's *not* a time warp. It's very tough, I think, to tell the audience that this is not a time warp when we are deeply involved with a subplot, which really became the main plot, in a holodeck image of

San Francisco, where bullets start flying and somebody gets hit and starts to bleed.

"That's pretty tough not to consider a time warp," he adds, "even though it was not. It was just an emotional and visual experience in the holodeck as equipment screwed up. I treated the two pieces as entirely different pieces. I did all of the 1941 stuff as if Picard is indeed playing Philip Marlowe, or rather the name they gave him: Dixon Hill, and play that for all it was worth as a genuine thing. The only key, the only balance, to keep the audience's memory of being on the ship is the dialogue that Tracy put in. There's a point where Captain Picard says to the doctor, 'We should be getting back to the Enterprise,' and she says, 'We're on the Enterprise.' He replies, 'Of course. It's becoming so real that I forgot.' That kind of thing.

"In this particular episode, there was far less of the futuristic space genre than there is on other episodes, which I made a point to see since the series started. We never looked out the window and saw other spacecraft or hostile whatevers...we were strictly on the bridge and down in the emergency area where the holodeck doors weren't functioning properly. In a sense, it was easy because I was able to do a 1940s picture, and went back only occasionally to the real story, which was the ship. But Tracy is the one who really made that happen. His writing, his structure, really made that possible. All I had to do was stay true to whatever period I was in."

As is normally the case with the average episode of the series, there are two stories going on concurrently.

While Picard and the others are trapped in the holodeck, Riker is forced to deal with the insect-like Jarada race who need to be greeted in their precise language by the captain so that the Enterprise can enter their area of space. If even the slightest syllable is missed, then they will be insulted and the Enterprise will be forced to go back the way it came. The time for the greeting is approaching, while the "search" continues for those personnel trapped in the holodeck.

Unfortunately, the Jarada never made an appearance in the final episode, although the audience did hear them.

"The budget would have gone sky high, so there was no way to do it," says Joseph Scanlan. "We shot it so that we heard this bug-like buzzing sound. We hear this strange, garbled, almost triple voice as described in the screen direction, but we never see them. Hopefully we were able to sell it that way."

The missing Jarada is the one aspect of the aired version that Tracy Torme is unhappy about.

"They were much more interesting in the script," he emphasizes, "and for budgetary reasons they ended up being a plot point. For instance, they're part of a hive-like race, so when they spoke you heard a man's voice, a woman's voice and a child's voice, all simultaneously. When the show aired, and that wasn't in there—they instead sounded like Alvin and the Chipmunks—I asked [co-executive producer] Rick Berman what had happened. He explained that it was done in post-production and they ignored my notes in the script. So, there are frustrations even in the best of experiences when you're a writer."

And, he emphasizes, the writing of "The Big Goodbye" was a wonderful experience.

"Gene wanted to utilize the holodeck and had thought of the idea of doing a detective story there," Torme explains. "I have always been a big Raymond Chandler fan, and even more of a *film noire* fan. So, I thought it would really be fun to do something like that, and 'The Big Goodbye,' more than any other script I've ever worked on for feature or TV, just fell into place almost magically for me. When I turned the first draft in, it's the closest I've ever been to being satisfied that I can remember. I just felt very relaxed about it, and believed that it was going to work. Some scripts are a struggle, while others aren't. This one was very definitely not a struggle compared to some of the others, so I have quite an affection for that show."

As well he should, considering that this particular episode went on to win the prestigious Peabody Award.

 Interestingly, there had been some talk that the Dixon Hill material would be shot in black and white, but that idea was quickly jettisoned.

"That was the first thing out of my mouth when I read the script and had my first meeting with Rick and Bob," admits Scanlan. "They said no, and Rick added, 'If it wasn't our own characters; if we were observing something back in the forties, we might consider it...but if Captain Picard and the other members of the crew 'go back' and turn black and white, and then come back out of the holodeck in color, it loses Gene Roddenberry's original concept of the holodeck.' That concept is that it's an emotional experience that starts visually and takes on an emotional reaction, but you never cease to be aboard the ship. You don't go back to 1941, you go to the holodeck on board the Enterprise. It's a fine line, but one that I obviously didn't feel strong enough about to argue with. Rick—he's a bright son of a gun—also thought that it was a little obvious; that we shouldn't do it. So we didn't."

Nonetheless, "The Big Goodbye" stands as one of the earliest bright spots in the show's first season, and a show by which others would be measured.

TWELVTH CHAPTER

For some reason, which this writer has not yet been able to discern, just about every science fiction television series an absolute necessity to do a story in which one of the main characters is split into two versions of him/herself, one good and the other evil.

That's a hell of a premise...once.

That's a heck of a premise...twice.

That's a boring, cliched premise...more than twice.

Yet the idea continues, never quite surpassing the first show to do it, **Star Trek**, whose "The Enemy Within" episode dealt with a transporter malfunction which split Captain Kirk into the aforementioned good/evil twins. The theme was brilliantly handled by all involved, wonderfully acted by William Shatner and has supposedly assisted in the treatment of mentally disturbed people.

Then **Logan's Run** tried its hand at the idea in an episode where Jessica is "copied" into an evil incarnation of herself who is determined to stop Logan from running.

Knightrider gave us an evil version of both the car, Kitt, and its driver, Michael.

V gave us the Star-Child being cloned by the evil Diana so that they could unlock the secrets of her DNA in order to develop a vaccine against the deadly toxin developed by mankind to get rid of the Visitors.

Then **Star Trek: The Next Generation** presented a variation of the theme with their episode "Datalore," which, despite being far superior to every version but the first the original **Star Trek**'s, still seemed repetitious, with an overhead view shot of the two Datas seemingly lifted right from the old show.

In that episode, the Enterprise travels to the world Data was created on, where they find a deactivated version of the android. They bring it to the Enterprise, put it together and activate it. This version, who refers to himself as Lore, seems even smarter than Data, and considerably more human, which ultimately turns out to be a drawback. It fills the android with evil and treachery, that leads him to nearly sacrificing the Enterprise to a crystal creature credited with destroying Data's world. Ultimately, it is a battle between Data and Lore, in which Data barely manages to prove victorious.

This is an exciting episode which gives actor Brent Spiner the opportunity to prove his varied talents by portraying two contrasting versions of the same character. Director Rob Bowman adds a healthy dose of suspense. In fact, the only drawbacks are several direct lifts from "The Enemy Within," the most obvious being that the evil Captain Kirk was scratched by Janice Rand, and he in turn scratched the noble Kirk to confuse the crew. Here, Lore has a facial twitch, which he gives to Data so as to mislead the rest of the crew.

"I would say the show was finally unlocking and moving ahead at that point," says producer Robert Lewin. "We had more freedom to work and the question is: with that kind of freedom, will we be able to get the excitement we want? I think to some degree it can, and that this show can appeal to the same audience that the old one did. But you've got to have tension, adventure and life-threatening situations. That mix is sometimes hard to get, but that's what we were trying to do; to make those characters irresistible."

An earlier version of this story, entitled "Apocalypse Anon", dealt with an Enterprise rescue mission of a doomed planet. A shuttle taken to the world's surface is captained by a Starfleet officer named Minuet, who Riker quickly takes a liking to and just as quickly falls in love with. He is eventually shocked to learn that she is an android, but this does not seem to alter his feelings until she points out their futility.

It's obvious this draft was an attempt to provide more depth to the main characters, which is certainly applaudable. Riker's irrational love for an android becomes the most important element of the story, surpassing the mission at hand. The character of Minuet, incidentally, would show up again in the episode entitled "11001001," as a holographic image that Riker falls in love with. In that story she is part of the programming supplied by the Binards, and used as a distraction so that Riker will not discover the aliens are kidnapping the Enterprise. In that situation the relationship works more effectively than it does here.

THIRTEENTH CHAPTER

Equal rights for all has always been an important part of the **Star Trek** mix, a point evidenced right from the beginning where Caucasians, blacks, Orientals, Russians, Scots and aliens worked side by side. Gene Roddenberry envisioned the 23rd Century as an era for everybody, with no one left out.

While it was certainly refreshing to see this approach continue with **The Next Generation**, an opportunity was missed to explore this theme on an even deeper level in the episode "Angel One." As aired, the story sends the Enterprise to Angel One in search of the crew of a freighter lost several years earlier. Data informs Captain Picard that on this world females are the dominant gender.

Riker and an Away Team beam down to the planet's surface and meet with the ruling class, expressing their desire to recover their lost comrades. The women are resistant to this idea, and we eventually learn the hu-

mans—led by Ramsey—were at first considered a curiosity, and then a threat to the societal structure of Angel One. Coming from Earth, they believed in equal rights for males and females, and were rallying support from the other men of this world, which would eventually lead to revolution. They were forced into hiding, and if the Enterprise can locate them, they are welcome to take them. For, as the leader points out, if they remain, they will be executed. Without breaking the Prime Directive, Riker and his Away Team must convince the government of Angel One that even the execution of these men will not extinguish the flames of revolution.

Running concurrently with this story is one in which a respiratory disease rapidly spreads throughout the ship, infecting almost everyone and leaving Beverly Crusher the task of finding a cure before it's too late. Frankly, this disease business is going a little bit too far. We've seen diseases spread across the ship in "The Naked

Now" and "Where None Have Gone Before," so it's already becoming old hat. In addition, the main plot seems too preoccupied with sex, rather than equality, which was its original intent.

"'Angel One' was about a reverse role society," explains Herb Wright, "in which women ruled and men are subservient. It's been done a thousand times already, including Gene's **Planet Earth**. So the major issue that we wanted to make sure was straightened was that I didn't want to do Amazon Women that are six foot tall with steel 'D' cups. My feeling was that the hit taken on this should be apartheid, so that the men are treated as though they are the blacks of South Africa. Make it political. Sexual overtones, yes, but political. Well, that didn't last very long. The sexual places it was dragged to were absurd."

As originally conceived by writer Patrick Barry, "Angel One" very much dealt with apartheid. This point is emphasized at the very outset of the proposed story, as Riker, Troi, Tasha, Data and an all-woman security team beam down. Naturally Riker is the first to speak to the world's ruler, Victoria, and he is immediately in trouble. Apparently it is against the law on this world for a man to look a woman in the eyes, and the sentence for touching a woman is death, which Riker engenders when he stops her from striking him. Weapons are levelled at the commander, but Tasha, who recognizes how this system works, uses her phaser to stun Riker, causing him to lose consciousness and collapse to the ground.

Wow, great opener!

While Data, being a machine, is deemed higher than a man and thus allowed more freedom, Riker is dressed in the attire of the slave class and thrown together with other slaves while Tasha, who has taken over the Away Team of necessity, works to locate the Federation personnel they are seeking. What they eventually discover is that the societal structure on this world is in a state of flux. The males have grown tired of their lower class status, and the time is coming for them to revolt. Eventually, the Away Team is able to locate the human leader, Lucas Jones, who is spurring the men into revolution. When brought before Victoria, he attacks her verbally and is killed by her for his troubles. No sooner has he fallen to the ground dead, than there is an explosion in the distance and then another. His death serves to rally the other slaves, who make their bid for freedom.

With this revolution in place—without the Away Team's instigation—they beam back aboard the Enterprise, where Picard is recovering from the disease discussed earlier, only in this version of the story, the captain alone is infected. Picard is concerned that the Prime Directive may have been violated in this instance, but Riker explains that the Enterprise served more as a witness to this uprising than an actual part of it. This seems to satisfy the captain, and the ship is off for its next mission.

All in all, Barry's version of "Angel One" surpasses that which aired, giving us a powerful allegory, and an opportunity to explore one of the great crises of humanity currently facing the world.

FOURTEENTH CHAPTER

One of the interesting things that began to happen in **Star Trek: The Next Generation** by the middle of the first season, was that the attempt to create a sense of continuity. This is evident in "11001001," in which the Enterprise locks into spacedock for a computer overhaul, and repairs of the holodeck which has "recently" malfunctioned. This malfunction refers to the mishap of "The Big Goodbye," in which crewmembers were trapped in a reality by the Enterprise computers.

This particular episode also serves as a highlight of the first season, and signifies a marked improvement in the quality of the scripts. In this case, the Binards— a race as close to living computers as you could find— work on the Enterprise computers.

While this is going on, the majority of the Enterprise crew and their families leave the ship for shore leave. Picard relaxes and catches up on his reading, and Riker, told by the Binards that the holodeck is repaired and enhanced, programs the area's computer to recreate a jazz bar, where he is given the opportunity to play the trombone. In addition, he is instantly captivated by a strikingly beautiful woman named Minuet, who seems perfectly made for him. Minuet, of course, is the name originally given to the android character in the first draft treatment of "Datalore." As Riker gets swept up in the atmosphere of this illusion, the Binards punch information into the computer and depart. Soon, Picard joins Riker, and is swept up in the vision as well, simultaneously taking note that Riker is getting carried away by his fascination with Minuet.

Meanwhile, a leak develops in the antimatter chamber, and Data has no choice but to order everyone aboard to abandon ship before imminent destruction. Moments later, Data asks the computer for the location of Picard and Riker, but is told that the ship is empty. The android finds this odd, but does not pursue it further until he and Geordi are beamed onto the starbase. After they arrive, the apparent damage to the engines repairs itself, and the Enterprise breaks away from the space station, before leaping into warp speed.

Picard prepares to leave the holodeck, but as he steps into the corridor, he hears the red alert signal. He and Riker quickly discern what has happened and transport themselves to the bridge, where they find the Binards in a death-like state. Their world had been threatened by a supernova, so they downloaded all information from that planet's memory banks into the Enterprise's computer—the only computer large enough to hold that vast amount of information—and hijacked the ship. Their home world survived the nova, and now the only way to insure the lives of the Binards is to "return" the information from the starship, reviving the planet's main computer. As no real harm was done, Picard says everything should be alright, although there will be a hearing.

With everything back in order, Riker returns to the holodeck seeking Minuet, but finds she is no longer in the computer's programming as she was created by the Binards as a distraction.

Overall, "11001001" is a terrific episode, with an imaginative new alien race and an original premise. Riker's relationship with Minuet, which could have been ridiculous, works effectively. This is one of the better episodes of the first season.

FIFTEENTH CHAPTER

*A*ging and mortality are nothing new to the **Star Trek** universe. We've seen the crew of the Enterprise encounter premature aging in the original series episode, "The Deadly Years," and cope with midlife crisis in **Star Trek II: The Wrath of Khan** and mortality in **Star Trek V: The Final Frontier.**

However, the first time the search for a veritable fountain of youth occurred was in **The Next Generation** episode "Too Short a Season." Captain Picard was given emergency instructions from Starfleet Command to proceed to a hostage situation, where terrorists demanded Admiral Mark Jameson come to negotiate their freedom from Karnas. Enterprise is to serve as the transport vessel.

When we meet Jameson, he's an 85 year old man, bound to a wheelchair by a crippling disease. He is accompanied by his wife Anne. Throughout the journey, he rapidly grows younger, due to a age-reversing drug obtained during a recent negotiation. The primary focus is on his gaining strength, the crew's reaction to this, and Anne's terror at watching her husband slip away from her.

Picard wants to know *why* Jameson would risk his own life with this dangerous drug, and why Karnas requested him. We learn from the mid-20s aged Admiral that forty years earlier he had a similar hostage situation to negotiate on Mordan, when Karnas demanded phasers and other Federation technology. Finding himself with little choice, Jameson agreed, but to maintain a balance of power, he supplied other factions on the planet with the same weaponry. Jameson falsified Federation documents to conceal this deed, and now it has come back to haunt him.

Reaching Mordan, an Away Team, which includes Picard, beams down and makes a rescue attempt, but things get botched up when Jameson is stricken with severe pain that racks his entire body. No sooner have they beamed up, then Karnas contacts them, stating that if Jameson is not beamed down to the planet within ten minutes, he will kill a hostage. Fifteen minutes later, another will die. Jameson weakly pleads that Picard beam him down, for he knows Karnas will free the hostages *if* he has the admiral. Moments later, Picard, Beverly Crusher and the young Jameson beam down, but Karnas refuses to accept the young man as the admiral. Jameson collapses once again, with Picard demanding Karnas recognize that this is indeed Jameson. He refuses, noting he wants Jameson to see the destruction and scars his actions from forty years ago caused.

Picard shows Karnas visual proof of Jameson's de-aging, while Anne is beamed down to be with her husband during the last few moments of his life. Jameson shows Karnas a scar he received during a private meeting between the two men; the blood scar that sealed their pact. Karnas pulls a weapon to kill the man, but decides not to, believing the man's suffering retribution enough. A moment later, Jameson dies. His need for revenge spent, Karnas states he will release the hostages.

For the most part, "Too Short a Season" is another fine example of what

Star Trek: The Next Generation should be doing, giving the audience believable characters and a highly enjoyable storyline. As is the case in most classic literature, Jameson ultimately pays the price for his attempts to tamper with nature, quite unlike the case of the original Michael Michaelian treatment and the first draft teleplay.

In that version of the script, Jameson pulled some strings at Starfleet to have Commander Riker promoted to Captain and assigned his own ship, so that Jameson himself could assume the role of Enterprise First Officer. Since Riker stays on as a consultant during this hostage situation, Jameson finds himself compelled to best the commander whenever and wherever he can. This includes deliberately excluding Riker from the Away Team by giving the man the wrong rendezvous time.

Karnas is known as Zepec in this version, and his decades old enemy is the High Priest. Picard and Riker use the transporter to arrange a meeting between the two men, and when they recognize they've been fighting for so long without ever having met each other, they come to the realization that the time has come for peace. Mission accomplished, and the Enterprise sets off on her way. But what of Jameson?

The de-aging has been different than in the aired version, with Jameson's aged and youthful personalities coming into conflict with each other; his behavior becoming more erratic and confusion replacing logic. He ultimately ends up 14 years old, and has no memory of his marriage to Anne. The proposed episode ends with Wesley giving the youth a tour of the Enterprise, and the young man's proclamation that he hopes to someday become a captain, like "Mr. Picard."

Frankly, it's better altered. In this version, Jameson actually seems rewarded for his actions 40 years earlier, and for cheating his wife of her husband. He is, in effect, given a second chance at life. Justice is best served in the Dorothy Fontana co-written teleplay.

"The high concept that Michael Michaelian came in with was male menopause," Fontana says, "which is a subject not often touched in television. Michael said, 'Well, I've been going through it lately, and I can really sympathize with the whole idea of wanting to go back to the man that he was, and coming to grips with the man that he is and will be.' It was interesting, but he wanted to do it with reverse aging; someone seeking out that youth for a purpose. Of course using a science fiction gimmick, you can do it in a matter of days. Michael did a treatment and a first draft script, but the key element that always went a little wrong with it was the terrorist angle; why we were going to that planet. The Macguffin. A lot of what I put in at the end was also in Michael's story and drafts, but approached with a different emphasis. Also, instead of it truly being terrorists, it's all a trap, pulling Jameson to the planet. Those were pretty much the changes."

SIXTEENTH CHAPTER

A primary difference between the Enterprise of the old show and the new, is that the latter carries entire families on a mission which supposedly will span some twenty years. When this particular point was originally announced, there was some concern there would be kiddies running all over the ship, but, thankfully, this has not come to pass.

Still, "When the Bough Breaks" focuses on the children of the Enterprise in a very touching and sentimental way. The ship picks up energy readings, equatable with galactic bread crumbs, that lead them to a mythical world known as Aldair, which Riker compares to the lost city of Atlantis. Unfortunately, the myth is much grander than the reality, as a pair of Aldairians materialize on the

bridge, preach friendship, and then ask Riker, Troi and Beverly to join them on the planet's surface. Once the trio have appeared there, the bombshell is dropped: the people of Aldair are dying, as there are no children. The adults have become sterile, and without aid their race will perish. They wish the Enterprise to leave some children with them, and in return will provide information that mankind will not learn for centuries. Naturally this is not good enough, as humans are extremely protective of their children. Since the answer is negative, the Aldairians do what any super powerful aliens would do: they kidnap six of the Enterprise children (including Wesley), and treat them as Gods so they will allow themselves to be assimilated into their culture and continue the race.

Picard makes an attempt to get them back, and in response the aliens propel the Enterprise some three days away and set up a force field. The Aldairian leader proclaims that if another rescue attempt is made, the starship will be pushed so far away that by the time they return, the children will be aged. In the meantime, a couple of the children seem to be adapting, while Wesley and several others prove resistant.

The Enterprise returns three days later, around the time Beverly discovers from medical scans that the Aldairians are dying from chromosome damage. With or without children, the race is doomed to perish unless she can find a cure. Meanwhile, Wesley speaks to the children, and convinces them to act completely miserable so that they can be returned home. The children embark on a hunger strike.

Picard and Beverly ask to be brought down, and while the planet's shields are lowered, Riker and Data beam down to the planet's main power source. The captain confronts the Aldairians with the fact that the children want to go home. They protest, but Beverly and Picard argue that they're suffering from radiation poisoning. The aliens are about to zap everyone away, but Riker and Data shut down the planet's main computer, making the inhabitants' equipment inoperative. The children beam back to the Enterprise while Picard and an Away Team point the Aldairians in the direction of self-discovery. Picard is willing to help in any way, including replenishing the world's ozone layer. In addition, Beverly reverses the ster-ilization, and we've got another happy ending for all.

As stated at the outset of this chapter, "When the Bough Breaks" works because it deals with an ignored aspect of the Enterprise. We also learn a lesson about blindly trusting technology. Incidentally, this episode was the first to use Wesley to best advantage since "Where None Have Gone Before."

SEVENTEENTH CHAPTER

Unfortunately, "Homesoil" falls short of the high standards established by the previous three episodes. Its greatest failing is its plot which seems to be a hybrid of several earlier **Star Trek** stories.

The episode opens with the Enterprise arriving at a world currently being terraformed by a group of scientists attempting to utilize Federation technology to bring life to a barren world. The process, and the description of it, appear to be taken directly from the Genesis Project featured in **The Wrath of Khan**. Then there are elements of the original series's "The Devil in the Dark" episode, in that the scientists are destroying life forms which exist on the planet. In the original episode, Federation miners were killed, and the "culprit"

turned out to be a moving rock creature known as the Horta, attacking because the miners were destroying its silicone eggs, although no one was aware of it.

The lifeform of "Homesoil" is a crystalline, intelligent being brought aboard the Enterprise and placed in the medical lab in a containment jar. Before long it splits into two entities, which communicate with the crew, referring to them as "ugly bags of mostly water." It continues to grow angry because the scientists have been destroying their kind. After the intelligence takes over the computer controls of the ship and it looks like all will be lost, a level of understanding is reached. The crystal-beings are transported back down to the planet, but not before they have the opportunity to call us barbaric savages, emphasizing that it will be three centuries before the Federation can return to the world.

Sorry, but it's awfully tiresome to constantly be called barbaric (hell, Q did the same thing in "Encounter at Farpoint").

Things improved with "Coming of Age," which gave us an interesting pair of stories. The first was Wesley's attempts to get in to Starfleet Academy, and the various tests he must undergo to gain entrance. These include technical exams, practical exams and the dreaded psych-test, in which all applicants must face their greatest fear. It's a close call, but, naturally, Wesley misses getting in by the barest of fractions, which is not surprising. If he had been accepted, the character would have had to leave the show. One thing that should be pointed out about this story is that it is another opportunity to show that in the right creative hands, Wesley can be more than an annoying teenager who always saves the ship. Wil Wheaton handles the part in such a way that you're actually rooting for the character by the end of the segment. Things were destined to improve for both the actor and character, particularly during the second season when the character was treated as a regular and not a boy genius who happened to be on the bridge.

The other story deals with Admiral Quinn and his assistant Remick, who beam aboard the Enterprise to conduct an inquiry into Picard's command abilities. Remick conducts indepth interviews with the various bridge personnel, asking pertinent questions which relate to a variety of past adventures, including the death of Jack Crusher and such episodes as "The Naked Now," "Where None Have Gone Before," "Justice" and "The Battle." After Picard has taken all of this he can, and Remick has not been able to prove any wrongdoing on the captain's part, Picard confronts Quinn and is told of a conspiracy in Starfleet which threatens the very foundation of the Federation. Quinn needs someone to trust in a position of power, and he wants Picard to take command of Starfleet Academy. Picard demands an explanation of the conspiracy, but there is none forthcoming, as the admiral eventually dismisses it as paranoia. Ultimately Picard refuses the potential promotion, emphasizing that his place is aboard the Enterprise. Quinn accepts this and departs with Remick.

While the investigation serves little purpose at this point, it is nice to see a sense of continuity between episodes. Take note that Quinn's concern regarding a conspiracy would return in the first season episode of the same name.

EIGHTEENTH CHAPTER

"I like to give Worf twists all the time," proclaims actor Michael Dorn, "and he has developed from a character who just grunts and growls a lot with a sarcastic one-liner kind of attitude to one who has turned out to be very complex."

Helping Dorn achieve this goal was the episode "Heart of Glory."

"I consider 'Heart of Glory' to be an information episode," he explains, "because it gave you everything you wanted to know about what happened with the Klingons. Why did they become allies? Why is Worf there? How did he get there? That type of thing. It was very good, although I felt it could have been taken a little further. What I wanted was an epic battle in the end, but it was a good show for me, because it showed them that people are as interested in Worf as they are in the other characters."

That "interest" is not surprising, particularly when one considers that

Star Trek's Mr. Spock was probably *the* most popular character of the original crew, due mostly to his alien nature. It would seem that that has a lot to do with Worf's popularity, as well. Season two of **The Next Generation**, in fact, has devoted considerably more air time to the Klingon officer than to many of the other supporting characters, and the rumor is that the third year will continue to flesh out the characterization, creating a strong Riker-Worf relationship along the lines of that of Kirk and Spock.

The Enterprise answers a distress signal from a Klingon ship supposedly attacked by a Ferengi vessel. Data analyzes debris, and announces the destruction does not appear to be the result of the Ferengi, although the Romulans are a distinct possibility. An Away Team transports over to a drifting freighter craft, and Geordi's visor detects structural weakness. A search for survivors continues, until they come across three Klingons, one of whom is seriously injured. Then everyone beams back aboard the Enterprise just before the freighter collapses.

In sickbay, one of the Klingons claims that the Ferengi attacked, but Worf points out that the weapons were not of Ferengi design. The Klingons seem to have an answer for *every* possible question. Picard dismisses them, and Worf escorts them to an eating area, where the Klingons immediately launch into a gentle, taunting assault on Worf, wondering how he can be so comfortable working with humans. Their conversation is interrupted by a communique from the captain, stating that the third Klingon is dying in sickbay, and there's nothing that Crusher can do to prevent it.

Later, after life has left the warrior's body, the two remaining Klingons continue their questioning of Worf, doing their best to incite his warrior blood and subtly imply that he should join a struggle against humans; pointing out that he should be among his own kind. Eventually—perhaps in an attempt to sway Worf —they tell him that they are the ones who destroyed the Klingon ship, because the rebels were going to be brought back to the Klingon home world due to their rebellious ways, and refusal to accept the peace between their people and the Federation.

A Klingon battle cruiser approaches the Enterprise, informing Picard that the Klingons on board are criminals, and should be transported over to the cruiser when they are in range. A security team is sent to the lower decks to bring the Klingons to the bridge, and Worf finds himself quite literally in the middle of the two factions. Ul-

timately he does not stop security as they lead the duo away to a holding area. It is a short matter of time, however, before they utilize hidden weapons to escape, killing one security guard, while one of the Klingons is killed in turn. The survivor makes his way to the engine room, where he proclaims that he will speak *only* to his countryman, Worf!

Worf goes to engineering, where he finds the Klingon aiming a weapon at the anti-matter chamber, threatening to destroy it if he is not set free. At the same time, he tries to sway Worf to his way of thinking, but Worf makes it clear that his loyalty is to Starfleet, as he fires his phaser, which unintentionally causes the other Klingon's death, leaving Worf alone to ponder his own heritage and identity.

Quite simply, this is an absolutely marvelous episode. Director Rob Bowman, who deserves a lot of credit for the skill he's brought to his **Next Generation** episodes, manages to convey a tremendous amount of suspense in what is the relatively confined space of the Enterprise. The script presents a tremendous opportunity to take an inside look at the make-up of the Klingons, moving them beyond the status of black hats, and Michael Dorn is given a chance to prove what all of us suspected all along: he is a truly gifted actor, and Worf is one hell of a character whose potential has not yet been tapped. Thankfully this would be corrected later on.

NINTEENTH CHAPTER

oming off of the success of "Heart and Glory," **Star Trek: The Next Generation** hit audiences with a one-two punch in the form of "Arsenal of Freedom" and "Symbiosis," a pair of stories which, like their immediate predecessor, demonstrated what this series *should* and *could* do, giving us exciting and thought-provoking stories coupled with great characterizations, and all delivered in an entertaining package.

"Arsenal of Freedom" provides a chilling and riveting storyline, involving the ultimate salesman: a computerized Peddler representing all that remains of a planet whose entire population consisted of arms dealers. Arms negotiations were their greatest strengths, but somehow their technology overtook their wisdom,

and they were destroyed, leaving only the automated weapons systems and the computerized Peddler behind.

The planet is Minos, and this is where the Enterprise has arrived in search of information to, or survivors of, the U.S.S. Drake, which mysteriously disappeared. An Away Team transports down to the planet's surface, and is immediately attacked by one of the automated weapons. This is disposed of quickly enough via a single phaser blast, but it is only a short matter of time before a second unit appears, and it takes the combination of two phasers to destroy it. What the team quickly realizes is that each time a unit is destroyed, the main computer assesses the situation and devises a replacement that can adapt to its opponent. Things go from bad to worse when Riker is suddenly held in a stasis-field. It takes concentrated phaser fire to free him.

Picard, who has been monitoring events on the surface, beams down with Beverly Crusher to see what aid they can render, while leaving Geordi in command of the Enterprise. No sooner have they arrived, than they fall into a deep cavern housing computer equipment. Unfortunately, Beverly Crusher is seriously injured, and the captain has to do everything in his power to keep her alive.

Meanwhile, in space, the Enterprise is forced to raise shields to protect itself from a planetary weapon system, which could conceivably destroy the vessel. Geordi has the saucer section separate and head towards the nearest starbase, while he and the remaining crew use everything at their disposal to destroy this automated enemy so that they can beam the Away Team, Picard and Crusher back on board.

Essentially, there are three stories going on: the Away Team's efforts to stay alive on the planet's surface, Picard and Beverly trapped underground and Geordi's situation aboard the Enterprise. Much of this abates when Picard is greeted by the Peddler, who is terribly excited about showing off the technology he has for sale. When the captain states that he has been convinced and will indeed purchase these weapon systems, the Peddler joyfully shuts the system down. Geordi, through clever maneuvering which includes bouncing the Enterprise off the planet's atmosphere, makes the planetary unit vulnerable to phaser attack and, then, destruction.

This terrific episode extrapolates on modern-day mercenaries and arms dealers. There is one complaint: initially the idea was that having Beverly and Picard trapped together underground would give them the opportunity to explore their true feelings for each other, but for one reason or another this was eventually dropped.

"Symbiosis" was also an exciting episode, in that it addressed a pertinent issue in a way in which **Star Trek** has always excelled. While studying solar flare activity, the Enterprise comes across an alien freighter in serious trouble. They beam four people and some cargo (which was transported in lieu of two additional crewmembers) aboard before the shuttle is caught in the sun's gravitational pull and destroyed. Amazingly, the two Aurelians are more concerned about the cargo than their lost comrades. Also, the two Brekkans continually emphasize that the "merchandise" (i.e. the cargo) is not theirs as of yet, and that payment was destroyed with the Aurelian freighter is of no concern to them.

After some time, we learn that the Aurelians' home planet is suffering from a plague that only the Brekkans can cure known as Felicium.

After careful analysis, Beverly discovers there isn't a plague. Rather, the Aurelians are addicted to Felicium, and *that* is the illness they suffer from when not given their dosage; they are plagued by withdrawal symptoms. It is the doctor's suggestion that she introduce an artificial substitute that will gradually relieve them of their dependency. Picard tells her that this is impossible; it would be a violation of the Prime Directive. These people, he reasons, have had this symbiotic relationship for years, and who are they to force *Federation* beliefs on them?

Picard and Beverly inform the Brekkans of their knowledge of the situation between the two races, but the Brekkans are thrilled to learn the Enterprise will not interfere. Picard still manages to come out on top, however, when he rescinds a previous offer to supply the Aurelians with coils their freighters need. By doing so he will eventually cause a breakdown of the system between the Aurelians and the Brekkans, resulting in the former's inevitable discovery that the plague does not actually exist. By *not* acting, the captain forces a change, without violating the Prime Directive.

This was certainly an intellectual approach to a heinous problem currently facing our society, and with the exception of a "just say no" conversation between Tasha and Wesley (though one can understand it's inclusion for the sake of children in the audience), there are absolutely no complaints about the episode. High praise should be given to everyone involved, and one can only hope future episodes will continue to address issues of significance to today's audience.

TWENTIETH CHAPTER

ypecasting has been one of the greatest problems facing the cast members of the original **Star Trek**, and it has undeniably affected their careers for the past twenty years. Perhaps this wouldn't be so terrible a fate, except, as many of them have rightfully pointed out, that they feel their contributions to actual episodes were limited to such lines as "hailing frequencies open," "Standard orbit, Captain," "Aye, sir," and the like. These are certainly not the kind of acting challenges that attract the attention of casting agents.

Naturally, the cast of **The Next Generation** shared similar fears, with the original cast's fates held out in front of them. Yet, while most of them have been pleased with the material they've had to work with, Denise Crosby felt portraying Tasha Yar was not all it had been cracked up to be. There simply was not enough time to give everybody equal time, thus the supporting characters had little more than supporting parts. She confronted

series creator Gene Roddenberry with these feelings, and was told point blank that Tasha Yar simply would not have much more to do in the future, so she asked for, and was granted, release from the series.

Now, Crosby's character *could* have merely been transferred to another vessel, as was the case with Beverly Crusher when Gates McFadden was fired (although she will be returning for the third season). Instead, the actress's departure was deemed the perfect opportunity to emphasize the danger that faces the crew of the Enterprise at every turn. It was mutually decided the starship's security officer should meet her demise, and the script chosen was Joseph Stefano's "Skin of Evil."

A space shuttle transporting Deanna Troi and a pilot to a rendezvous spot for pickup by the Enterprise runs into mechanical interference and is forced to crashland on a planet. By the time the starship arrives, the worst is feared. Scanners indicate the shuttle to be covered by debris that the transporter cannot penetrate, so an Away Team must transport down and make a rescue attempt. Shortly after materializing, however, they have trouble getting to the shuttle due to what can only be described as an oil slick that blocks their path at every attempt to pass. The slick rises into a somewhat solid form, and one of the first things it does is strike out at the woman, sending her reeling lifelessly to the ground. The Away Team immediately beams back to the ship, and Beverly does her best to bring Tasha "back," but to no avail. As she describes it, the slick sapped the life right out of her. Because of the possibility that Troi is alive, they beam back down to the surface, and confront the slick once again.

It rapidly becomes apparent that this being is pure evil, taunting the Away Team in vicious and childish ways, and constantly reinforcing the idea that they are fragile things he can destroy at whim. They want to recover their comrades from the shuttle, but even this will not be allowed by the compassionless creature. Picard eventually beams down and confronts the creature, learning that it is the result of a race of people who brought everything dark and evil from within themselves to the surface and cast it out of their bodies, thus creating this being of unadulterated evil. It wants out of this place, and will allow the captain to get Deanna and the pilot *if* the Enterprise provides transport. Picard agrees in principle, and finds himself within the shuttle.

Meanwhile, Worf and Wesley devise a plan to simultaneously beam the Away Team and those people in the shuttle up, noting that when the creature uses its abilities, the power source blocking the transporter beam weakens. The plan works, and everyone returns to the Enterprise, which breaks orbit and leaves the creature behind for all eternity. Picard's log states he will warn Starfleet Command to put this world off limits to all other vessels. The episode concludes with a funeral for Tasha Yar, and a holographic message that she left behind for her comrades in case she should die while on duty.

While this episode works fairly well, and Tasha's death is handled wonderfully, the biggest problem is the creature itself. It looks like nothing more than a man in a rubber suit covered with oil. This, in turn, takes away from the overall impact of the show.

"When you read the script," explains director Joseph Scanlan, "it has a wonderful intellectual quality to it, forgetting the complications of creating the creature. This entity had such an ironic quality. I thought his dialogue was extremely interesting and found his one on one with Picard to be the ultimate face off. I was very enthusiastic about doing it.

"When I was talking to the producers," he continues, "I said, 'If we don't make this monster believable, we are in deep water, because this could be a most wonderful concept, but he's a very sympathetic character.' It was important that we not have the audience feel sorry for him when it's over, but I would guess that if you and I took a poll, half the audience would feel great empathy for him. The poor guy is there in this little puddle and that's that. I think the producers really wanted him to be so evil that you'd say, 'Leave him there. F——k him,' but of course it never happened that way. There was no way to avoid empathy for him, which led to the irony of the situation. He killed Tasha, he damn near killed Riker, and I still wasn't mad at him. Look at what his people had done. How could you *not* feel sorry for him?

"If we had a four million dollar budget and were doing **Alien**, we had the potential for a very intelligent piece of work. But to do it in seven days is very tough. My first cut was just barely adequate, and it took input from the producers to make it better. I had always wanted a Roddy McDowall-type of venomous evil coming out of the mouth of the guy, but the producers leaned more towards what you got, which was the throaty presence, but always somewhat ominous. The bottom line is that it became a caricature, I think, and as a result, as close as it came to being a good show, it was not a good show. Unless you sell the audience on the black blob, you're dead. You've got this blob of oil to deal with. Sometimes all it's doing is vibrating down there, sometimes it's waist high, sometimes he's out. You *know* there's an actor there, which is the long and short of it. Of all the shows they did, 'Skin of Evil' was probably only on the top rung of the second half. It was like 45 percent out of 100 percent. There were some shows that were bad because they weren't conceived properly. This show, conceptually, could have been wonderful, and the only reason it wasn't, and it was nobody's fault, were the pressures of time and budget."

It's unfortunate, but the next episode of the series, "We'll Always Have Paris," was something of a disappointment. The plot deals with the time/gravity experiments of Doctor Paul Manheim, which has resulted in a rip in the dimensional fabric. The tear is causing the present and the future to intermingle at certain moments, resulting in time distortions which could expand to a galactic level if the planetoid, if the equipment is not shut down. Combined with this is Manheim's wife, Jenice, a former love of Picard's, who is aboard the Enterprise because her husband seems to be dying. As the man eventually explains it, it's as though his mind and soul are sharing two dimensions at one time. It comes down to Data using the doctor's information to shut down the experiment, while attempting to cope with three versions of himself from different time continuums, all of whom are trying to decide which Data should actually carry through with the shutdown, as it calls for a precise timing.

It is tough to pinpoint the exact reasons this show doesn't work. Perhaps it has to do with the relationship between Picard and guest star Michelle Philips as Jenice. Also, the time displacement story, while featuring interesting elements, does not come across clearly. Why, for instance, should other dimensional copies of the main characters appear, but only for a moment? Logically, they should remain, resulting in numerous copies, making the story even more convoluted. "We'll Always Have Paris" should be chalked off as a fascinating idea that just didn't come together.

TWENTYFIRST CHAPTER

"I wrote 'Conspiracy' with the idea of doing something different; something with an unhappy ending, a harder edge, elements of horror," states writer Tracy Torme. "I thought that even if people hated it, the show would be back to normal the next week. I wrote it intentionally to be different, *hoping* that it would cause controversy."

Torme got his wish. "Conspiracy" is a standout episode of **Star Trek: The Next Generation**. Picking up on threads laid down in "Coming of Age," Picard is contacted by Captain Walter Keel of the starship Horatio, who has Picard meet him and several other starship captains on a remote planet. There—after testing Picard's memory—they inform him of a conspiracy within the Federation. The words almost duplicate the warning given to the captain by Admiral Quinn in "Coming of Age." Picard has a difficult time believing, but is convinced when the Horatio is mysteriously destroyed.

Later, Data is told to investigate all recent Starfleet communiques, and learns there does seem to be an attempt to solidify certain sectors of Federation space. Picard now recognizes the potential threat, and orders the Enterprise to Earth, where he will confront the head of Starfleet Command to get some answers. Upon arrival, Picard and Riker are told to beam down to Earth in twenty minutes, while Admiral Quinn states that he would like to be brought up. Picard sees this as a hopeful sign, that Quinn is still on their side. Unbeknownst to Picard, Quinn has brought a briefcase containing a scorpion-like creature.

On the Enterprise, Picard asks Quinn about the conspiracy theory, but the man brushes it off as the captain reading far too much into his words. The captain and first officer separate from Quinn for a moment, with the former stating that somehow this man is *not* the real Quinn. Picard wants Riker to stay aboard to keep an eye on the man, while he beams down to Starfleet for his meeting. There Picard greets the Federation council and Commander Remick, also from "Coming of Age."

Riker goes to the observation lounge, where Quinn is waiting, and is told that in the man's briefcase is a unique life form. Riker doesn't want to take a look at it, but Quinn forcefully insists, throwing the commander around the room as though he were a rag doll. Riker contacts security before he is rendered unconscious. A moment later, Worf and Geordi arrive, and are quickly disposed of as well. Before Quinn can depart, Beverly arrives and fires a phaser at the man. Shockingly, it takes several bursts before the man is rendered unconscious.

In sickbay, Beverly performs an examination, and states that the man before her is indeed Quinn, but obviously there is something different about him. Then, attached to the man's neck, she finds a small, quivering object that resembles a worm. When contacted by the captain, she tells him of the parasite, and the distinctive mark on victim's necks and that phasers must be set on kill to have effect.

Picard joins the council for dinner, and finds a bowl full of worms. Nauseated, the captain stares at the others devouring the live creatures, while they explain they are aware of why he is there. While they don't answer many questions, they do state that conquest is foremost on their mind, and humans are such easy targets. He moves to leave the room, when Riker walks in, stating that it will only be a short matter of time before Picard is one of "them." One of the council members checks the commander's neck, and sees the tail of a parasite. Everyone sits at the table and prepares to eat, but just as Riker is about to devour a handful of worms, he whips out his phaser and fires at one of the council members, then another. As they fall to the ground, the scorpion-like parasites crawl out of their mouths and make their way down the corridor. Riker and Picard follow one of the creatures into another room, where they see it enter Remick's mouth. With little choice, the duo open fire with phasers, ripping the man's chest open, causing his head to explode and revealing a mother creature, which they next destroy. This has the effect of curing everyone who had been possessed.

The episode ends with many unanswered questions, and the unsettling announcement by Data that Remick had sent a homing beacon to an unexplored sector of the galaxy. This may someday allow the parasite race to travel back to Earth to make another attempt at conquest.

Interesting to note is that in the first draft teleplay, the parasites did not enter Remick. Instead, Picard and Riker went into the outer room, where they found a giant creature—actually thousands of the smaller creatures grouped together as one—sending out the homing beacon, before they destroyed it with their combined phaser fire.

Needless to say, even in its aired form, "Conspiracy" is one hell of a **Star Trek** episode. It is different from any that had come before or has been aired since. Combining the show's premise with a healthy dose of **Invasion of the Body Snatchers** or *The Puppet Masters*, Tracy Torme gave audiences a chilling example of what the series was capable of.

"'Conspiracy' began as a show they had called 'The Assassins,' which had gone through a few drafts and was really not close to anything they wanted to do," explains Torme. "I agreed to take it over, with the condition that I could really turn it upside down and basically create a new story. Originally, I had made it a **Seven Days in May** kind of story with a coup inside Starfleet by various officers who felt that the Prime Directive was too restrictive, resulting in the Federation getting too soft. They believed that peace with the Klingons had made us complacent and somewhere down the line there would be a threat we would be unprepared for. The coup's leaders were all Picard's friends. I really liked that story, because it had nothing alien in it at all. It was about paranoia. Gene rejected it. He liked it, but didn't want to open that can of worms.

"So I knew the story had to change," he elaborates. "Then, I realized that this was the next to last show of the season, and I really felt that although the series had improved a great deal, we were still too comfortable and weren't pushing the limits of what we *could* do. Thanks especially to [then producer] Robert Justman and Rick Berman, who really got behind it, 'Conspiracy' kept 95% of its original hard edge, and because of that, it is a special show for me. I'm proud of **Star Trek** for being willing to take a chance. Die-hard fans who want a nice, neat and comfortable universe at all times, might be a little upset, but that's okay."

Unfortunately, things became a little too neat beginning with the next episode and through part of the second season. In addition, there has been no mention of the parasites since, which is truly a pity, considering the impact that this episode had.

TWENTYSECOND CHAPTER

I n March of 1988, Holly-wood was hit with a major strike by the Writer's Guild of America. It crippled the television industry. There was a mad scramble by the studios to complete their quota of episodes for the season.

The result can be seen in **The Next Generation**'s season finale, "The Neutral Zone," a hybrid of two scripts which do not come together.

The Enterprise finds an ancient spacecraft from Earth that contains cryogenic freeze units housing human beings. They are brought aboard the starship, and Beverly states that each of them had been dying, and were put into deep-freeze until a cure could be found for their illness. Somehow they broke Earth orbit and have been drifting ever since. Beverly cures these people of their ailments, and then the task becomes one of assimilating them into the 24th Century, which is not an easy thing since this group consists of people that live on Earth in our present day.

In the meantime, the Enterprise is investigating the destruction of several Federation outposts near the Neutral Zone, and they suspect the Romulans. During a tension-filled (and terrific) final five minutes of the episode, a Romulan vessel appears, its commander stating that they had nothing to do with the destruction of the outposts, as they have been busy with "problems" of their own (which one can assume would be the parasite threat from "Conspiracy"). Their final words are chilling: "We are here to serve notice, Captain. We're back!"

Frankly, those last five minutes should have been the episode's teaser, with an Enterprise/Romulans tale following the commercial break. Instead, we have a tired and silly retread of the original show's "Space Seed," that serves little more purpose than to provide comic relief. Certainly not an auspicious way to conclude the season.

EPILOGUE

As Bob Lewin stated near the outset of this volume, every television series goes through a shakedown period when the cast and crew struggle to find the show's strengths and weaknesses.

In the case of **Star Trek: The Next Generation**, it's safe to say every episode was at least competently made, and quite a few *attempted* something new and dynamic in terms of story and character development, but very few actually made the grade. Of 24 aired episodes during the first season, only a little more than a fifth could be considered strong, while a little more than that can be deemed good efforts, with the rest ranging from mediocre to fair. This may not seem a terrible overall ratio, but the number of successes is disappointing. One must ponder the reasons.

Is it just that good, solid scripts weren't available? This doesn't seem likely, as many unproduced stories and earlier drafts of produced episodes were superior to the aired episodes. Were special effects and set design a particular problem? No, the effects and basic sets of **The Next Generation** are, quite frankly, gorgeous, surpassing anything done in the field to date, thanks mostly to Industrial Light and Magic handling the former, and the set designers who made the Enterprise appear to be a functional spacecraft. Combined, these elements present a very realistic view of what the 24th Century may look like.

What then is the problem? Perhaps it all stems from the attitude, "if it ain't broke, don't fix it."

The original **Star Trek** was a survi-vor. Like the fictional hero Rocky Balboa, the series managed to go the distance; for three seasons struggling to remain on the air against seemingly overwhelming odds, including network censorship, poor time slots and low ratings. The series was *forced* to survive or perish. The choice was as simple as that, and for that reason those laboring in front of and behind the cameras did their damndest to make the show *different* from anything else on the air. The scripts were literate and the ensemble a realistic "family" of characters. The audience constantly felt **Star Trek** was trying harder than anyone else to deliver quality television.

Star Trek: The Next Generation, conversely, has it too easy. It exudes confidence that cast and crew *know* the show is going to be a ratings success. For the most part, there doesn't seem to be any challenge to produce scripts that delve into ideas which different than what's come before. The show suffers from familiarity.

Writer Tracy Torme, who has gone from Story Editor to Creative Consultant on the series, succinctly sums up **The Next Generation**'s problems: "It would be nice if people started taking more chances with television, because we're *barely* scratching the surface of its potential," he says. "The medium does very well covering sports and news, but when it comes to drama, it was better 20 or 30 years ago. Everyone is looking for formula, and that really gets boring after a while. The opportunities are there, if you're allowed to take advantage of them, to really do something different that will shake people up a little bit, but hardly anyone is doing that."

Including, he notes, **Star Trek**.

"The format of the show opens many of those doors, but then it's up to **Star Trek** to be bold enough to *do* something unusual, challenging or artistically stimulating," Torme points out. "Having the opportunity doesn't mean you're going to fulfill the promise. A conservative approach was taken, that has carried on to this day, of not rocking the boat too much; not taking too many chances. My position on this has been pretty well known. I'm the one person who tries to push to do unusual, unexpected or, hopefully, progressive things on the show, but there always seems to be resistance. It always seems to be a struggle to do something that's ground-breaking. Again, that's because the show is such a success that the attitude has become, 'Why take risks?'"

The lack of risk taking became apparent again during the show's second season, where the series quite amazingly followed the pattern set by the first. It began very weakly, the stories picked up steam towards the latter part of the year, and have varied in quality ever since.

Series creator and executive producer Gene Roddenberry has stated that he wants the third season to be the best year for **Star Trek** *ever*, and at this point we can only take a wait-and-see attitude, although, as fans, we want the show to succeed greatly, and boldly go where **Star Trek** has not gone before.

APPENDIX

APPENDIX THE LOST EPISODES

Through the course of every television series, there are numerous teleplays or treatments which are developed but never make it to the air. Sometimes this is attributed to the quality of said storyline, which may not be up to par with the rest of the series, while at other times it has nothing to do with the quality of the tale whatsoever. Perhaps there are political motivations behind such decisions, or perhaps what was written would have exceeded by far the allotted budget for an hourly episode. Whatever the reason, locked in the vaults of every production studio are numerous stories which were purchased and never taken any further.

Why, you might ask, would anyone care. Frankly, the answer to that depends on the television show in question, and if that show happens to be Star Trek, then it's pretty easy to assume that there is a great deal of fascination regarding the tales of the starship Enterprise which have never made it to the air.

Trek: The Lost Years, also published by Pioneer Books, provided an in-depth look at the years between the cancellation of the original Star Trek and the announcement of the first feature film a decade later, while serving as a guide to the scripts and treatments written during that period. But now, with the advent of Star Trek: The Next Generation, there are even more proposed fables of the 24th Century which there would generally not be access to...until now.

This portion of the text provides a guide to some of the unused stories written for the first season of The Next Generation. Are they better off remaining in the vault, or would they still make terrific episodes? You be the judge of that.

"BLOOD AND FIRE"

If there is one script of **Star Trek: The Next Generation** which has garnered more attention than any others, it would have to be David Gerrold's "Blood and Fire."

One aspect of the original **Star Trek** that has allowed it to withstand the passage of time was its uncanny ability to produce thought-provoking storylines in an entertainment format. By the same token, **The Next Generation** has provided plenty of entertaining stories, but very few, with the exception during season one of the excellent "Symbiosis," have touched on pertinent issues. "Blood and Fire" was Gerrold's attempt to do so, tackling head-on the AIDS virus and our reaction as a society to it. While the script does have problems (arising from the supposedly cryptic homosexual relationship between two guest stars not being as subtle as the author would have liked), it fulfills its promise.

"Blood and Fire" begins with the Enterprise approaching a scientific research vessel known as the U.S.S. Copernicus, which had sent out a distress signal and is now adrift with no further communication. An Away Team beams over, and is horrified to find many lifeless bodies, apparently drained of their blood. Geordi's visor detects quick glimpses of wavicles, but they are gone before he can study them further. Ultimately Beverly Crusher, who has been tracking the Away Team's progress, realizes that the crew must have become infected with bloodworms, a life form that spreads so quickly — and so deadly a manner —that Starfleet's standing orders are to never attempt rescue of a vessel whose crew has contracted them.

Eventually Beverly derives a cure, in which all of the blood is drained out of the victim's body, killing the bloodworms, and then replaced by an artificial substance. While Beverly beams over to the Copernicus to try out her cure, Data informs her that the bloodworms were created as a doomsday weapon to be used in a Regulan war. Ultimately Beverly and the others come to the conclusion that the bloodworms are desperately trying to metamorphosize into another life form, but something in their genetic make-up is preventing the transition. Using plasmasites and a human volunteer/ sacrificial lamb, they are able to aid in the transformation of the bloodworms into a "beautiful glowing cloud of color and light and flickering sparkles." As they reach the next step of their evolution, what had once

represented horror and death, is now a thing of beauty and a source of awe.

David Gerrold, known throughout fandom as the author of "The Trouble With Tribbles," recently spoke at a **Star Trek** convention, discussing his involvement with the new show, as well as the genesis of "Blood and Fire."

"The title of this talk is 'Blood and Fire — The Script You Won't See on **Star Trek**,'" Gerrold told the audience. "I have to do this very delicately. It was said of me last week that I never wrote anything useful for **Star Trek: The Next Generation**, because I'm too old to write for **Star Trek**, which I thought was a rather remarkable thing to say, particularly coming from the man who said it. I thought, 'You could insult me as a person all you want, and I'll probably agree with you, because I know what it's like to live with me. But when you talk about my passion for writing and the quality of my writing, then you're talking about something serious.' I thought what I would do is talk to you about how this script got written, what's in it, and I will let you judge for yourself if I'm too old to write for **Star Trek**.

"**Star Trek: The Next Generation** was announced on October 10th [1986], and I was hired on October 20th,

and was immediately involved with a lot of development work. I wrote the first draft of the bible for Gene and I also did the final draft, and that was probably one of the most exciting and happiest experiences I had working on the show. Gene and I had long meetings about the characters, who would do what and how it would work out. At that time, Gene was a writer's dream of a producer, because he was available for input, listening to things people said and incorporating lots of good suggestions. As we started going, Gene suggested that I start thinking of story ideas, which I did.

"I don't know how other writers work, but let me tell you how it happens with me. There are things I want to write about and things I want to address, and sometimes they all fall into the same story at the same time. One story I started thinking about dealt with a planet of very religious, puritanical people and we have an observer living on that planet pretending to be one of them and they're about to burn him at the stake. In order to rescue him, we accidentally beam up not only him, but several people who are about to light the fire. Of course they end up in the transporter room, and all of these very religious people think that they've been transported to heaven.

The problem for the Enterprise was going to be, 'How do we tell these people the truth without violating the Prime Directive and shattering their religion and culture, and how do we return them without also interfering with their culture?' The idea being that if we send them back, they can say they've been to heaven and have seen God. So we were working on that idea, and Dorothy Fontana suggested that the story be postponed, and that was because some of the other stuff we had in the works was a little soft and she thought I should work on the action story I had also been playing with.

"What I wanted to do was deal with Regulan Bloodworms, because we had mentioned them in 'Trouble With Tribbles.' People were always asking about them, but who knows what a Regulan Bloodworm is? At that particular time, there was a lot in the news about the AIDS panic and people not donating blood. Blood donorship was a major issue for me and always has been, and to hear that donorship was down because of fear of AIDS exposure, I wanted to do a story where at some point maybe the Enterprise must roll up their sleeves to donate blood to save the lives of some of the crewmembers. I thought, 'There's an interesting idea for a sto-

ry.' So that was floating around in my head. Also, we had had a discussion of whether or not we could use Mike Minor as our art director. Unfortunately, Mike was very sick with AIDS at the time and has since passed away [as has actor Merritt Butrick, who portrayed Kirk's son David Marcus in **Star Trek II: The Wrath of Khan**], which is a great loss to us. He worked on the **Star Trek** features, and had been involved in many different ways. I thought, 'Here's an issue we really ought to address.' I thought I would do a story that asked the question, 'What do you do with an infected population?' All of this is floating around in my mind. But let me give you the rest of the source material.

"In November of '86, we all —Gene and I, George Takei, Robin Curtis and some others —were at a convention in Boston called Platinum Anniversary. It was a 20th Anniversary celebration, and they had invited us all before they knew there was going to be a **Star Trek: The Next Generation**, so we all went out there and they were thrilled, because we were able to talk about what we planned to do on the new show, and they were very excited.

"There is apparently a gay science fiction club in Boston and they said, 'Gene, we've always had on **Star Trek**

in the past minorities clearly represented. Isn't it time we had a gay crewmember on the Enterprise?' He said, 'You're probably right. Sooner or later we'll have to address the issue and I'll have to give serious thought to it.' I thought, 'Okay, fine,' because I was sitting in the back, taking notes. Whatever Gene said was going to be policy. We came back to Los Angeles and I'm still making notes for the bible and other things, and we're at a meeting with Eddie Milkis, Bob Justman, John D.F. Black, Gene and myself, and Gene said, 'We should probably have a gay character on **Star Trek**. We seriously have to be willing to address the issue.' So I said, 'Okay, now I know that Gene seriously meant what he said in Boston, and I know that that's story material we could do.

"At that time, I felt very positive, because by saying we could do that kind of story, Gene was also indicating a willingness to do a whole range of story material. As a writer I was excited, not just by that particular idea, but by the whole range of story ideas that were available. All of this is floating around in my head. I wanted to do a story that somehow acknowledged the AIDS fear, something with blood donorship, and I started blocking out a story called 'Blood and Fire' about Regulan

Bloodworms, and where it started was with the idea that we find a ship that has been infected, and if you have a starship that is infected, what do you do without bringing the infection to your own ship? I thought we should make it a really horrendous thing that there's a standing Starfleet order that when you run into a ship that's infected with bloodworms, the order is to destroy that ship immediately, because (a) it is the merciful thing to do and (b) the last three ships that tried to save an infected population were also infected and died horribly.

"In the first few stories written, we saw that they were a little soft and there wasn't much action, and to balance that I wanted to do a show that had a lot of hard action and adventure in it. So the idea is that they could find another ship infected with bloodworms and they have a major problem, and to make it even more serious, first the Away Team beams over and then they find out that the ship is infected with bloodworms. Now we have a problem. That's where I started, then I worked out the lifecycle of the bloodworms, that they grow in your blood until they reach a certain point and then, like malaria, they explode and start looking for new flesh. It was a very graphic kind of

suggestion. I had a lot of fun with it, Dorothy liked it and Herb Wright loved it, saying that it was the kind of story we needed to do.

"I knew there were going to major questions that you, the audience, would be asking about the new show, so I wanted to address a couple of those concerns. I was having some fun with the script based on some of the things that you had been asking at the conventions.

"There is only one scene that deals with the relationship between Feeman and Eakins [the gay characters], and if you don't know better, they're just good friends. I wrote that in a way to acknowledge the contribution that gay people have made to the show and acknowledge that they were all taking a large part of the burden for the AIDS epidemic, because this story was an AIDS allegory. Then we deal with blood donation.

"It's a very grim story and had it been shot the way it was written —or shot at all — there's a very satisfying ending that is truly a **Star Trek** ending, and part of it is that we don't truly understand who or what the bloodworms are, and there are things we don't understand that we have to learn. I won't spoil the ending by telling you what it is. I'm very pleased with the script. When I finished it, I felt

that it represented some of the best writing I'd ever done for any television show anywhere, and I thought it could be a better episode than 'The Trouble With Tribbles.' Not as funny. I wanted to do something distinctly different from 'Trouble With Tribbles' and this is it. I turned it in and went off on the first **Star Trek** cruise and got a telegram from Gene that said, 'Everyone loved your script, have a great cruise.' When I got back I found that the script was cancelled. That's what I was told by someone who was in a position to know. I don't have any proof in writing, so I have to qualify it by saying someone told me.

"So it was cancelled for reasons that had nothing to do with its quality. It was just put on a shelf. I was very hurt and very upset about it, and the only way I can share it is to allow you go decide for yourself if this would have been a good **Star Trek** episode."

Producer Herbert Wright, on Gene Roddenberry's insistence, took to the script next, initially working closely with Gerrold on a rewrite.

"I was given David Gerrold's script to rewrite," says Wright, "but from all the notes I could tell that it was going to be a no-win situation. I talked to David about it and said, 'Look, why don't I write another script on a similar premise?' So I wrote a brand new script for them."

The result was "Blood and Ice," which followed similar story beats but dealt with a conspiracy on the part of the Romulans and several humans to unleash the bloodworms in Federation territory, resulting in the deaths of millions. The real difference between the two versions is that those people infected with the disease essentially become space zombies, with a penchant for blood. Gone, for the most part, is the AIDS allegory, and in its place is a straight tale of horror that reads like "Star Trek Meets Night of the Living Dead." And yet while the changes are many, it doesn't take away from the fact this this is one hell of a suspenseful and scary teleplay. Frankly, Gene Roddenberry and company would do well by taking both the Gerrold and Wright drafts of the story, and grafting them into a two hour episode. It would undoubtedly be an unforgettable experience.

"THE BONDING"

In "The Bonding," the Enterprise is in the midst of negotiating a peace treaty between two Federation planets which have developed a conflict with each other. Then Picard is abruptly told to abandon his mission and investigate civil disturbances on Omega Croton IV, and supply transport of refugees to a medical base. Enroute, Data states that the people of Croton are a humanoid race who are a part of a superior form of artificial intelligence. The nature of this sudden revolt is unclear.

Later, the refugees are brought aboard the Enterprise, and an elderly woman moves away from the crowd to place a Croton infant in an air-duct, and then wills the life out of her own body. Within the air-duct, it's obvious that this infant and the starship's computer have somehow linked, as the latter emits a gust of warm air, and follows with a "web-like diaper," which covers the child's bottom.

After the refugee transfer has been completed, Enterprise heads back to its original mission. On the way, however, the old woman's body is found, and Beverly Crusher quickly discerns that she was actually a member of the subject class surgically altered to look like a Croton. Why she wanted to come aboard the Enterprise is the mystery. Things get worse when Picard tells Geordi to fly the vessel through an ion storm, and the ship's computer alters course on its own, pointing out that *its* child may have been injured by such an attempt.

The boy is eventually found in the air duct by Tasha Yar, and brought to sickbay for examination, where they learn it is now approximately eighteen months old. Then, reality is really stretched by the author when the crew is able to watch what the deceased old woman had seen during her past few hours, thanks to the marvel of 24th Century technology. The images reveal the woman at a Croton temple, where she is handed an infant. The temple then explodes, and she hides the child beneath her clothing, making a desperate run for it. Further information obtained indicates that this child is named Pattrue, and he is the ruler of Croton. This is all verified by the boy, who is now ten years old, and extremely intelligent and articulate. According to the treatment, this boy possesses computerized intelligence and in an emotionless tone he asks to be granted political asylum. Essentially he wants to remain on board the Enterprise until the revolution at home settles down. The captain, trying to take all of this in, claims he will consider it.

Panic sets in later when it becomes obvious that something is draining information from the ship's computer. The search concludes with Pattrue, who is floating in mid-air, accumulating data. Riker tries to shut the computer down, but is unable to do so as the device explains the people of Croton are isolationists, and their society has been slowly deteriorating due to the lack of new informational input, which is why the revolution on the part of the Subjects is taking place. By gathering information in this way, Pattrue should be able to correct the situation. Data does his best to reassure everyone by pointing out that the computer is sharing information, not losing it .

Word eventually reaches Picard that the Subjects will end the revolution *if* Pattrue returns to Croton, but the boy stuns everyone by saying he does not wish to go. He has been gaining an understanding of emotions, and cannot go back to a world of machine-like beings. By story's end, Pattrue realizes that the greatest gift of humanity is selflessness, and he must go back home to impart the wisdom he has gathered.

Quite frankly, "The Bonding" doesn't really work, and one can see why it wasn't taken any further than the outline stage. While the basic idea of Pattrue is an intriguing one, the story doesn't make good use of him. Besides, the idea of a cold and logical being seeking and ultimately discovering the value of

emotions is an old one in the **Star Trek** mythos, and will never be done better than in the form of Mr. Spock.

Interestingly, the image of the old woman smuggling the infant on board the Enterprise so that he will, in effect, lead his people to freedom, is very much like the story of Moses as presented in **The Ten Commandments**. Also, the idea of an infant rapidly aging to a child would eventually be used in the second season premiere episode of **The Next Generation**, "The Child."

"TERMINUS"

Enroute to deliver medical supplies to Bynax II, the Enterprise receives a distress signal from Ty Norsen, who claims that the planet is in extreme danger. Warp speed is increased, when scanners pick up an unidentifiable object which is approaching. Scanners indicate that it is mechanical in nature, and its speed is increasing. The object passes the starship and is gone.

Enterprise arrives at Bynax II, and finds that there are no life forms evident on the planet. An Away Team beams down, and quickly comes to the conclusion that the lack of people, coupled with the earlier distress signal, indicates that something terrible is happening. They eventually learn that the people are un-

derground, having been instructed to go there by Norsen who warned them of great danger and destruction. Riker wants to know what's going on, but neither he nor Picard can get information out of the uncooperative Norsen. What Picard really wants to know is how Norsen had been able to send a distress signal *before* there had been any danger.

The mysterious object appears in space and stars scanning the planet. Norsen demands that the Enterprise provide protection, but then the object vanishes again. Both Picard and Troi consider the possibility that Norsen is being controlled by an outside intelligence. Norsen rebukes this claim, pointing out that his prediction of danger from this object (which has begun to bombard the planet's surface with gamma rays) has turned out to be correct, although he never explains just how he was able to come to this conclusion ahead of time.

While all this is going on, Data has been acting very strangely, causing concern among his shipmates. Quite stunning to everyone is the discovery on the planet's surface of another Data, and after the two androids speak and are brought to the bridge, some answers finally emerge. What they discover is that the object on the planet's surface is an exact duplicate of the device which had created Data on his native world, and has actually played a large hand in making Bynax II a habitable world. Apparently there are many of these devices located at strategic points throughout the universe, all doing their best to help humanity, who they admire very much. One of these devices had been destroyed by humans on a faraway planet and this race, angered by such an action, sent out a duplicate to hunt down the responsible people to extract revenge. Unfortunately something went wrong with the programming, and that particular object just continued in its mission to wipe out human life forms.

The communicating ability of the objects reached the one stationed on Bynax II, and the only way for it to communicate the threat was to "influence" Norsen's thinking patterns by giving him the image of the imminent destruction, thus allowing the man to lead the colony underground before the object arrived to unleash its wrath. When the message wasn't clear enough, it created a copy of Data, the only other machine-image it was aware of and this version was given the task of warning everyone that the device was headed their way.

Data II utilizes the creations of Wesley Crusher, and together they serve as a decoy for the returning object, which bombards them with gamma rays. While this is going on, the Enterprise opens fire with photon torpedoes, destroying it instantly. With the threat gone, Norsen leads the colony back to the surface, where they will rebuild, aided by a new android: Data III.

"Terminus," like quite a number of produced episodes, is only a mediocre offering, being neither overly terrible nor good. One must bear in mind, however, that this is only an outline and that the story would have eventually been refined and fleshed out had the production team decided to take it further. It would seem that elements of this story found their way into other episodes. Most notably, the duplicate Data idea appeared in "Datalore," and the alien-object element that reproduces itself, threatening a planet as well as the Enterprise, resurfaced in "Arsenal of Freedom."

"SOME WHEN"

The Enterprise is responding to a distress signal from a passenger ship called the Pleides. Their heading is the Docleic Triad, which is essentially an outer-space equivalent of the Bermuda Triangle, where a wide variety of ships have been lost over the years. Data explains that scanners indicate that an ion storm had recently passed through that area of space. Past studies of the area have revealed that the effect of such storms is to create "an electromagnetic 'waterspout' effect," which has been powerful enough to destroy vessels. The sensors indicate a phenomenon termed spheres within spheres, which are a series of "rings" made of energy. The situation is a dangerous one, but should they proceed? As the distress signal continues from the Pleides, the captain realizes that there is no choice. They must continue their mission. The ship is put on full alert, while at the same time Tasha's console alerts her to the fact that holodeck 1B is being utilized without authorization, but there is no one there. Worf is sent to investigate. Finding nothing out of the ordinary, he contacts her, states that the unit is not being used, and walks away. Then we "see a glow of light from the holodeck," and the image within shows Tasha adorned in a futuristic bathing suit, in the midst of a wild beach party.

As the Enterprise enters the Docleic Triad, we learn that Picard is being driven in part, by the fact that the next day is the anniversary of Jack Crusher's death. While the Jack Crusher connection is an interesting one, we're never really given the reason for its presence here. What does the Pleides have to do with his death? From what we know, the Stargazer (the vessel on which Picard and Crusher had served together) did not enter the Triad, so it's difficult to discern the connection between the two.

Meanwhile, in her quarters, Beverly, too, is reflecting on Jack's death, staring at a holographic photo of the man, and feeling sorry that Wesley never really got to know his father. Back on the bridge, and after the Enterprise has entered the first ring, Geordi stuns everyone by saying he's picking up readings for the U.S.S. Orion, which was a starship that vanished in the Triad a decade earlier. The ship is just hovering ahead of them, covered in a green glow. Communication and tractor beam attempts prove fruitless, as though the Orion isn't really there. Then, Enterprise is set aglow with the green light, but Picard orders the ship onward.

While Data and Geordi sit at their usual positions, an ensign approaches, asking Data to sign a report. Surprisingly, neither have ever seen her before, which is particularly strange in Data's case, as his computer memo-

ry recognizes every member of the Enterprise crew. She reminds Geordi of someone he had been attracted to at the Academy.

As Enterprise broaches the next ring, Beverly is in the midst of eating a meal alone, but hears a male voice state that he has just the right wine to go along with it. Beverly looks up, to see Jack Crusher sitting across from her. It turns out that Beverly and Jack are in personal quarters, but unlike any found aboard the Enterprise. As Beverly discusses a baby she delivered that day, Jack asks if she's sorry that they never had children of their own. She replies in the negative, pointing out that their careers are more than enough.

Picard, Riker and Data head for the ready room. Data is the last †o enter, and is surprised to find a bearded Picard talking to his first officer, Jack Crusher. The two men toast their ship, the Stargazer. Data moves back onto the bridge, where everything seems to be as it should be. As the starship enters the third ring, Geordi spots two other vessels, which Data concludes are the Androcles and the Utoria, both glowing as red as the Enterprise itself. A channel is opened to the ready room, and Picard and Riker return to the bridge in response. Data is, naturally, relieved. They try to raise

the two vessels, but are unable to do so. There are no life form readings on either.

Analyzing all the available information, Data comes up with a theory in which members of the Enterprise crew are ceasing to exist —at least partially —which is why communication with the other ships has been impossible. Picard is confused, wanting to know what he's talking about. Data responds that time is altering, and if they do not find the Pleides quickly, the ship will undoubtedly be lost. Then the Enterprise passes into the fourth ring, resulting in Picard's disappearing from the bridge. A computer search reveals that the captain is unreachable in the science analysis lab. Annoyed, Riker orders Data to find the captain and bring him back to the bridge. To make matters worse, the signal from the Pleides is beginning to break up.

Enroute, Data sees Geordi with the ensign we had seen earlier, but he is *not blind*. He makes it to the lab, but when he steps through the door he finds himself in Picard's quarters as seen in "The Battle," the captain holding a brandy glass and once again bearded. Data backs out of the room. Picard steps out a moment later, the beard gone, but still holding the brandy glass. Data, without saying anything, asks that he report to the bridge. Picard arrives at the exact moment that the Pleides is spotted on the viewscreen, both it and the Enterprise enveloped in a blue glow. The signal from the ship finally stops.

Data steps off the turbolift, telling them that they must leave this area of space. Picard is adamant that they not desert the people on board the ship, but the android points out that they are not picking up life form readings, which means that they and the Pleides are on different dimensional, or time continuum, levels. In addition, the longer they remain, the stronger the chance that they, too, will cease to exist. Things continue to get worse with the announcement that a second ion storm is headed toward them and will arrive in two hours, which might prevent their ever leaving the Triad.

Beverly and Data are trying to detect life forms on the Pleides, but all they're detecting is the machinery —no organic life. Data theorizes that machines remain constant, whereas people make different choices, thus altering their lives. Somehow that has become relevant in this situation. Beverly is fascinated by the idea that parallel universes exist (although **Star Trek** fans have known that since the original show's "Mirror, Mirror" episode), and the thought

that she might exist somewhere else. Wesley pipes in that "it's more like *somewhen*."

Picard gives Riker the helm as he departs the bridge, and a moment later the commander is referred to as captain by Geordi. Somehow time has altered again, and Riker is the captain of the Enterprise. Meanwhile, Data is enroute to the bridge when he peers in an open door and sees a beaten and bloodied Tasha Yar coming before a judge on her home world, and being sentenced to die. Realizing that another timeline is effecting this one, Data continues, passes the real Tasha and then finds a third one, who is this time a judge playing God with a prisoner. Realizing that three timelines are coming together, Data hurries to the turbolift. Another time flash, and we see a married Geordi raising a family, having never joined Starfleet. Elsewhere, Picard enters the observatory lounge, and warmly greets Beverly and Jack Crusher.

Both Data and the real Picard enter the bridge simultaneously, and Riker tells them they must abandon the Pleides immediately, as the second ion storm will definitely strike them if they do not get out of the Triad. After much internal debate, Picard gives the order, but the instruments under Geordi's control do not respond correctly.

Moving back in the

direction they came is difficult, but made slightly easier by Wesley's suggestion that they use the ship's they had spotted earlier as signposts which will eventually lead them out. Enterprise passes the Androcles and Utoria, and Data says he wants to make one more study of the time alterations throughout the ship, and leaves the bridge. Moving quickly, he discovers that as Enterprise makes her way back, parallel "worlds" are beginning to collapse, with things returning to normal. He sees true love between an alternate Riker and Troi reverting back to professionalism, and so on.

Enterprise approaches the first ring as fear of the ion storm grows. Wesley is about to offer his opinion, when he suddenly disappears. Computer search confirms that neither he nor his mother are on board the ship. Troi believes that Beverly wanted her life with Jack so badly, that she undoubtedly "willed or wished" herself into a life with him, which would mean that Wesley does not exist. Picard, believing that the boy's survival is absolutely vital, orders the ship back into the Triad so that the two will once again exist.

After quite a bit of searching, they come to the parallel world where Picard, Jack and Beverly are serving on the Stargazer. He must somehow speak to her and convince her to alter her own reality. He details the events of the real Beverly's life on board the Enterprise. Jack doesn't want to lose her, but she continues to sway back and forth trying to make a decision. Suddenly Wes appears, then disappears again. "We love you," Picard tells her. Wes appears again, with mother and son locking eyes on each other. Ultimately she chooses her son's reality. Jack disappears just as Wesley materializes completely. Beverly steps into her own timeline and the three of them head for the bridge.

Once there, the Enterprise is ordered out of the Triad at maximum speed, which is accomplished thanks to Wesley's contribution (although we're never told what it is). Through the rear-view screen, the Enterprise crew, now safe once again, stares at the electromagnetic phenomenon of the ion storm they've just avoided.

"Somewhen" has a damn interesting premise, but as presented in this form, it just seems too convoluted to have worked. There is so much happening that to cram it all into the forty-odd minutes of an average show could result in nothing more than a cursory treatment of the subject matter. In addition, we've already seen brief moments of fanta-

sy brought to life in several episodes, most notably "Shore Leave" on the old show, and "Where None Have Gone Before" on the new. In fact, there are even elements of "City on the Edge of Forever," what with Beverly having to choose between one life or another —in effect, deciding whether her son or her husband should die. While this was a valiant attempt by the writer, it's probably just as well that it didn't make it to the air.

"THE IMMUNITY SYNDROME"

The S.S. Beagle is in its death throes, the captain of the vessel stating as much in his log, pointing out that death is their only hope for freedom. Every hatch explodes out, taking the atmosphere from within with them. As the author notes, "the S.S. Beagle dies, preserved for all eternity in the empty void."

Picard's log informs us that the Enterprise is bringing supplies to the Beagle, but all contact was mysteriously lost and attempts at scanning have been fruitless. Their only hope is to go to the ship's last reported position to save anyone who might be left. Riker puts the ship on full alert, and tells the captain that he's needed on the bridge. Once Picard ar-

rives, he's told of the status of the Beagle, and that there is no damage to the ship. He in turn says to prepare an Away Team, which Riker does, consisting of himself, Beverly, Geordi and Data.

The Away Team beams over in "form fitting spacesuits —the latest in 24th Century technology." As the team breaks up, Data, Geordi and Riker proceed to the bridge, where they find a body frozen to a chair (as a result of depressurizing). Riker asks Geordi to try and bring the ship's engines back on line, while Data moves over to a console and realizes that every aspect of the ship's computer memory was frozen solid, its information irretrievable.

In sickbay, life support has been restored, and Beverly removes her helmet, as does her assistant, Ames. Riker then enters the area and is led to a frozen body, its chest exploded open. There is frozen blood everywhere. Beverly chalks it up to "explosive decompression" as a result of the ship's hatches being blown. Riker nears the body, but is told to stay away from it, as a risk of contamination exists. It is Beverly's opinion that the hatches were blown in an attempt to destroy *something* which would have proven deadly to much more than just the crew of the Beagle.

Shortly thereafter, the Away Team reappears on the transporter platform aboard the Enterprise. They are decontaminated, and then step off of the platform. The bodies of corpses are placed on futuristic gurneys, with Riker telling Beverly that he wants a full report upon the completion of autopsies. She acknowledges the order, then notes that Ames doesn't look well, to which the man replies he has a difficult time handling death. Beverly tells him to report to sickbay after completing his reports.

In the captain's ready room, Riker has detailed their discovery to Picard, who muses that the lack of personnel on the Beagle may be because no one had returned to it. Perhaps they had beamed down somewhere in the Aldebaran system and brought back a contaminant with them. They transported back down to find a cure, but were never able to make it back. Turning his attention to Geordi, he has the man set about retracing the Beagle's route.

Back in sickbay, Beverly examines Ames, but chalks up his reaction to seeing death, and nothing more. Physically he seems to be alright, but she recommends that he come back to see her again in two days.

On the Bridge, Geordi tells Picard that thus far they've been able to narrow the trajectories of the Beagle down to twelve hundred. Then the captain contacts sickbay, wanting a progress report from Beverly, who explains that the only cause of death was the explosive decompression. There is *no* sign of an inside influence which may have caused the ship's captain to blow the hatches. Riker is hooked on the idea of a contaminant, but admits that there really isn't any proof of such a disease.

Elsewhere, Wes is trying to involve Ames in a game of chessdroids, but the other man isn't interested, exploding that they're in the middle of nowhere and the only thing keeping them from the harshness of space is the bulkhead of the ship that they occupy. Ames insists that the Enterprise crew is going to end up exactly like the Beagle's. A fight develops between them, but two crewmen come over and break them up. As the struggle grows more serious, Wes contacts security and then sickbay, requesting a medic. In sickbay, Beverly is amazed at the change in Ames, noting that his white blood cell count is way above where it should be, but her real concern is over the way he's acting.

Picard, Riker, Beverly and Troi meet in the bridge lounge, with the captain trying to determine just what is going on with Ames. Riker starts to cough, which immediately draws the doctor's attention as commander is one of those people who *never* get sick. Picard is suspicious, wondering if anyone else who boarded the Beagle is coming down with anything, but he's told that there isn't. Beverly suspects that a disease is spreading. Troi disagrees, pointing out that they were all decontaminated when they beamed back aboard the Enterprise. "You can't decontaminate yourself for something you don't know exists," Beverly bluntly snaps back. Picard agrees, stating that the boarding party will have to be quarantined, but the doctor says it's too late for that. If there is a disease, it's already started to spread. She does, however, want the Away Team to report to sickbay for examinations. Picard orders Geordi to go to sickbay and after a moment's hesitation asks Wes to take over the task of limiting potential trajectories of the Beagle.

In the midst of examinations in sickbay, Beverly asks Riker what he had for breakfast, but the commander can't come up with the answer. She then asks Geordi some trivia, which he answers immediately. He, then, can go back to his station, but Riker cannot return to the bridge. Riker and other members of the Away Team are told that they'll be prepped for surgery, based on what Beverly discovered during the last phase of the autopsies performed on the Beagle crewmembers. The doctor explains that she wants to perform a brain scan on Riker, and he muses that the cure is worse than the disease.

"Patients always think that way," is her response. "Especially ones with an exaggerated sense of self-importance."

"What's that supposed to mean?"

"It means this ship will survive without you for a while."

This passage of dialogue was reprinted because it rang so true to life, and would be a welcome exchange between the characters, striking a chord of realism akin to the old **Star Trek**. Simple, but effective.

Suddenly there is a scream from Ames, but by the time Beverly has arrived, the man is in the midst of a massive coronary, and all attempts to reverse it prove fruitless. Riker looks on in horror.

Summoned to sickbay, Picard learns that the captain of the Beagle was suffering from a brain infection, which resulted from a reduction of immune abilities. Beverly terms it a cancer of the blood which eventually results in death. Using a medical device, she punches up the image of one of the dead men's insides, showing the green areas which indicate places attacked by the virus. When the hatches of the Beagle were blown, not only were the bodies frozen, but so was the virus itself, which was unleashed when brought into the warmer atmosphere of the Enterprise. It is her belief that the virus can survive in the atmosphere for approximately two hours. Apparently the other ship contracted the disease while in the Aldebaran star system, which is probably the only place that they'll be able to find a cure. Picard asks her if she's alright, and the doctor replies that she's a carrier without any of the symptoms. So far Ames and Riker are the only others infected.

Picard returns to the bridge, where the computer has finally been able to trace the trajectory of the Beagle. A course is laid in, and Enterprise is on her way. Going back to sickbay, the captain checks on Riker, who's growing weaker, and more paranoid, believing that they're all going to die. Beverly comes over with a hypo to calm him down, but the commander states they're trying to kill him. She's eventually successful, and Riker passes out. Then there is the sound of a struggle from another area of sickbay, where a crewman is screaming out that he won't let the "witch" use her black magic on him. Two members of security try to hold him at bay, but it isn't easy. One of the men explains that they caught this person with a thermite grenade, about to kill himself. Beverly tells them to strap him down in the ward. Beverly fears things will grow worse before they get better, with the captain pessimistically wondering if they will ever get better.

Enterprise is locking into orbit around Aldebaran IV, while Data starts to scan the planet. Tasha interjects that there are problems with various crewmembers on several decks. Beverly adds that there are twelve cases already in sickbay, and that they're beginning to lose control. Meanwhile in sickbay, Riker asks Davis, a med-tech, for some water, and tricks the man into opening his bonds. The commander immediately dispatches him and is on his feet, "a maniacal grin on his face."

Ship scanners have detected a nuclear power source, which Data deduces to be a man-made structure. Beverly believes that that is the key they've been searching for, and with Picard's permission, she has Data organize an Away Team, all of whom beam down mere moments later.

On the surface, they discover a research hut which was constructed by the crew of the Beagle, and within they discover three mummified bodies, which are deemed to be the other members of the Beagle crew. Back on the ship, Davis comes to and tells Tasha what happened, and she, in turn, alerts security that the commander must be captured. Meanwhile, Riker dispatches someone else and steals the man's phaser before continuing on his journey through the ship.

On Aldebaran IV Data suggests they burn the bodies to prevent the spread of disease, and Beverly concurs. While he sees to it, she goes back within the hut and grabs various tapes and slides, which she crams into a viewer. Later, Picard contacts her and she explains that the Beagle crew had found a planet which might be able to reverse the effect of the virus, but they ran out of time. She is going to try to finish what they started. Picard only asks that she hurry, as things are getting out of hand on board the Enterprise.

On the Enterprise Riker enters auxiliary control, dispatches the guard on duty and starts maneuvering various controls. On the bridge, Geordi receives an alert from the engineering deck. Tasha picks up on it, stating that auxiliary control has been "locked off," with the bio and warp systems being controlled from that area. Geordi informs them

that there is no way to override it, and Picard tells Tasha to have a security team meet him at auxiliary control. Arriving there, the captain begs Riker to let him in, but the commander merely argues that they're all dying, and he's just helping everyone out by speeding up the process. Picard wants the doors to the area blown open, but one of the security guards states that doing so would prove damaging to the guidance control computers. He slams the man against a wall, demanding that he follow orders, and then pulls back as he realizes what he's doing. Regaining his senses, he tells the man to get a plasma engineer to cut through the door.

On the planet, Data watches the flames which have engulfed the three bodies they had discovered. He then steps within the research hut, only to find that Beverly is starting to fall under the influence of the disease, chastising him because he supposedly thinks he's above them all; because he's not dying like the rest of them. Data suggests that she not lose control, which she somehow manages to agree with. There is an alarm from a computer she's been working with, which indicates that her experiments are complete. She removes a vial of green fluid, and has Data inject it in her arm, which results in

her collapsing to the floor.

Beverly comes to with Data's assistance. A blood sample is taken, and they discover that the virus has been destroyed by the vaccine. She tries to contact the Enterprise, where, on the bridge, Geordi states that their orbit is starting to break up due to what Riker's been doing. Beverly gets through on a rapidly disintegrating communication channel. Picard orders the transporter room to beam up the Away Team. Word comes from the transporter room that the Away Team is aboard. Wes approaches Picard, stating that he has come up with a theory which will allow the Enterprise to sling-shot its way across the atmosphere of the planet, and then allow them to break out of orbit. The captain accepts what the boy has said, and his plan is put into motion. After an extremely dangerous moment or two, the starship ends up in space again, having narrowly avoided destruction. Then, Riker, who had been hauled out of auxiliary control, enters the bridge, trying to place himself under arrest for mutiny. Beverly follows him, stating that he's going with her, and the two depart with Data. In the turbolift, Beverly apologizes for what she had said to Data on the surface, while on the bridge, Picard congratulates

Wesley for his plan. Geordi states that the ship's warp engines are back to full capacity and, bearing that in mind, orders the Enterprise to engage its engines at warp one.

The title of this script, "The Immunity Syndrome," is the same as one of the original show's episode, which was a mistake on the author's part. In addition, the plotline of this story is *very* similar to **Star Trek**'s "The Naked Time," and **The Next Generation** remake, "The Naked Now," with a disease rapidly making its way through the Enterprise, altering the personalities of crewmembers and causing someone (in the former Kevin Riley, in the latter Wesley Crusher) to lock themselves off in a section of engineering and play havoc with the ship's engines. Yet despite all this, "The Immunity Syndrome" is a terrific script, and probably would have been a vast improvement over the aired version of "The Naked Now." The author proves himself more than competent in handling the **Trek** universe, and most definitely deserves the opportunity to try his hand at another story. This tale is a riveting one, and the treatment of the characters is absolutely terrific. You really do believe just about everything they're saying, and we are made privy to some inner conflicts between them, which would have been welcome on the series itself.

"THE CRYSTAL SKULL"

Arriving at the desert planet Bolaxnu 7, located mid-way between Federation and Ferengi territory, the Enterprise is assigned the task of bringing supplies to an archaeological mission being led by Doctor Annette Boudreau. Elevating this mission above the mundane is the doctor's announcement that she has discovered a lost city which indicates that this world is actually Izul, of the Faran Empire, which mysteriously collapsed over eight thousand years earlier.

An Away Team consisting of Riker, Data, Worf, Wesley and Beverly and a med-tech appear at the threshold of a pair of monoliths, which create a passage into the aforementioned city. Taking in their surroundings visually and via tricorder, Riker opens up a channel with the Enterprise and instructs the transporter room to beam down the supplies. Moments later five supply modules materialize, just as Boudreau and two members from her team "appear" at the entrance. The woman's beauty touches Riker. After introductions are over, she explains that a man named Roark was

recently injured and she's concerned about him. When it's pointed out that Beverly is chief medical officer of the Enterprise, Boudreau leads her and Riker through the entrance and into the subterranean room, where the injured man lies. While the doctor is off taking care of him, Riker asks Boudreau about Izul, but is told that her proclamations may have been premature. Before the commander can discuss the issue further, she excuses herself.

Shortly thereafter, Riker is walking through an underground tunnel where he encounters Data and Worf, who have overseen the transfer of supplies. Data is particularly intrigued by this discovery, explaining that a distant colony of the Faran Empire which was stranded after it collapsed, was the Ferengi home world known as Bunol. This discovery could, theoretically, provide some tantalizing information pertaining to Ferengi culture. Reluctantly, Riker tells the android of Boudreau's claim that she may have been wrong in making the announcement in the first place. His curiosity piqued, Riker excuses himself and makes his way down to the doctor's chambers, where he sees her sitting down grasping a crystal skull, while apparently in a meditative and ecstatic state. As

Riker enters the room, she starts shouting that he should leave and not come back, but he refuses. He wants to know what the skull is. While ordering him out, she moves to put the skull in hiding, but Riker reaches out, touches it and suddenly begins to smile as he pulls the skull from her hands.

All of Boudreau's attempts to take the skull back prove fruitless, so she gives in and asks Riker if he's going to share it with her. He says that he will in his own good time, and then starts to kiss her passionately. Needless to say, things aren't exactly right with the good commander.

On the Enterprise bridge, Geordi informs Picard that what appears to be a Ferengi ship is approaching. Looking to Troi for some kind of an answer, the Betazoid only tells him that she can feel obsession, but doesn't know where it's coming from or what it pertains to. Considering all of this, Picard contacts Riker, informs him of the Ferengi vessel and states that the Away team should be ready to beam up at a moment's notice.

Back on the surface, Boudreau is concerned that the Ferengi are out for revenge against them because of the historical value of this place. Riker tells her that everything is going to be fine, as he places

the skull in a leather bag and embraces her. Later, the two of them proceed to the subterranean chamber we had seen earlier, where they join the rest of the Away and archaeological teams. Once there, Data begins to discuss the connection between the Ferengi and the Faran Empire, as well as the philosophy of the Faran's emperor, Doshin, who was, according to the treatment, "actually a succession of rulers, all of whom took the same name and had one thing in common: the possession of a crystal skull said to have mysterious powers." All of these emperors of Izul did a great deal of writing, which added, in some part, to the formation of the Ferengi society. An additional fact supplied by the android is that the Ferengi took to Izul in the same way that Earth people took to Camelot, with the skull, then, being an equivalent to the Holy Grail. Turning his attention to Boudreau, he asks if she is at all familiar with the legend of the crystal skull, to which she responds in the affirmative, although it is her understanding that it was destroyed thousands of years ago.

Picard contacts Riker, telling him that due to the denseness of the tunnels, the transporter is unable to lock on to the archaeologists, and the signal from the Away Team is extremely low. The Ferengi are

still approaching, so they have to beam those people with communicators up first, and the rest must proceed to the surface where sensors will be able to lock on to them. The channel closed, Riker places his communicator on the injured man, and then asks Worf to place his on Boudreau, which the Klingon does. Although Wes wants to give his insignia to an archaeologist, his mother points out that the boy has never had any training in combat. Riker agrees, so Wes, Beverly, a med-tech, Boudreau and the wounded man are beamed up, with Riker telling everyone else that they're going to have to move up to the surface.

The Enterprise has received a communique from the Ferengi vessel, captained by Zaeb, who claims that Picard is heading a spy mission. Actually amused by this claim, Picard asks him how he came to this rather remarkable conclusion, and Zaeb responds that they had picked up a transmission from a Federation "agent" named Boudreau, who bragged over her discovery of the crystal skull. This is followed by the proclamation that the planet now belongs to the Ferengi, and all members of the Federation had best vacate it. Picard counters that since his people were the first to chart this system, it should belong to the

Federation. This is interrupted by Geordi, who announces the beam-down of a Ferengi landing party. Turning his attention back to Zaeb (and sounding very much like our old friend James T. Kirk), the captain warns that if harm should come to *anyone*, the price extracted will be a high one.

Making their way through the tunnels, Riker and company run into the Ferengi landing party and the "blue-skinned Oriental-looking Kakiri Warriors," who level their weapons at our people. Riker merely smiles in response.

Luug, the commander of the Ferengi team, tells Riker that he and his people are now prisoners of the Alliance, and instructs them to turn over their weapons. Riker's response is to laugh, as he confidently replies that he knows that the Ferengi have come for the crystal skull, an item which he has already obtained and hidden. Any moves on the part of the Ferengi or the accompanying warriors will cause Riker to trigger a thermonuclear device he has hidden in the underground realm (although "thermonuclear" would be an archaic term by the 24th Century, and the Ferengi should have sensed that Riker was bluffing). The commander adds that Picard must take part in the final negotiations which will occur

within the hour. Luug, not wanting to chance losing out on the skull, agrees to Riker's terms. Turning his attention to Data, Riker tells him to move everyone else outside so that they can be beamed up. The android is also instructed to have Captain Picard and Doctor Boudreau beamed down in an hour.

Once everyone but Worf has gone, Riker turns to the Klingon and instructs him to check on the "device," which Worf, going along with Riker's plan, turns to do. Once he is alone, the commander turns back to Luug and tells him that he and Picard would be interested in some "goodwill unofficial trading" that would make the crystal skull seem like a mere trinket. He goes on to impress the alien by speaking of Ferengi philosophy, and as the conversation develops there seems to be a chord struck between these two.

On the bridge, Data has detailed Riker's instructions to Picard, who is confused by all of this. The only way to get the answers he needs is to beam down to the planet's surface (although, bearing in mind everything this new series has set up, this simply would not take place. The captain, under no circumstances, would put himself in such a hostile situation until Riker himself had confirmed the safety of the planet).

Back on the planet, Worf compliments Riker concerning the way he handled the Ferengi, although he is a bit bothered that the commander had essentially gone against honor codes taken at the Academy by lying to the Ferengi about their possession of the skull and the thermonuclear device. While this seems a serious point with the Klingon, Riker brushes it off, chalking it up to a plan that he has, which will be explained to Picard as soon as the captain beams down. Changing the subject, he tells Worf to check some of the back tunnels to see if they might possibly lead to the surface, so that they have an escape route should something go wrong with the scheduled meeting.

Shortly thereafter, Picard, Troi, Tasha, security agents and Boudreau appear in the underground chamber, and are surprised to find neither Riker or Worf anywhere. The captain calls out, not realizing that Riker is currently in Boudreau's quarters, the skull in his hands and his expression betraying a meditative state. But Picard's voice cuts into his concentration, and he places the skull back in the leather shoulder bag, which he hides elsewhere. From there he steps into the central hall where everyone is waiting for him. Boudreau runs up to him and wants to know if what she's heard regarding the Ferengi and the skull is true, but Riker merely smiles at her reassuringly. When Picard wants some answers, the commander side-steps, merely stating that the two of them and Data will be the only ones involved in the negotiations. No security and no Betazoids. Boudreau will also join them, as she has a working knowledge of the planet and its history.

Back in sickbay, Roark comes to for a moment, looking at Beverly and saying something about the crystal skull and that a woman must be stopped. Unfortunately the doctor cannot make any sense out of this statement. We shift back underground, where the group is about to be left alone. Before the others go, Riker approaches Troi and tells her that there is something he wishes to speak to her of; feelings he wants to express that he has never been able to express before. Then Picard says it's time for them to proceed. The remaining members of the group start making their way through the tunnel, when Riker suddenly knocks out Data (exactly how is never explained), and Boudreau takes care of the captain. Their communicators and phasers are taken. Boudreau is delighted, pointing out that they will have the

skull to share between the two of them. Riker, unfortunately, has other plans, as he knocks her out as well. Leaving the area, he utilizes his phaser to create a cave-in that effectively seals everyone within.

Riker moves back into the doctor's quarters where he retrieves the bag containing the skull and moves out of the area. Moving into the outer chamber, he encounters Worf, who has joined up with the security team, and explains that the Kakiri betrayed them and murdered Picard, Data and Boudreau. Saying that they have no alternative, Riker has them beamed back up to the Enterprise.

Back on the bridge, Worf is absolutely furious at what has happened with the Ferengi. Riker does his best to placate him, while ordering Geordi to raise the Ferengi captain. Zaeb's image appears, and Riker angrily chastises him for the attack on personnel from the Federation. Naturally the alien has no idea of what the human (or human, as they like to say) is talking about. Riker's curt response is that the Ferengi ship had better surrender within ten minutes, or it will be destroyed. The channel is closed, and the ship is brought to red alert status. Certain members of the bridge crew take note that he seems to be *anticipating* the imminent battle.

Underground Data awakens, and quickly revives the captain and doctor, as all three try to figure out exactly what happened. Boudreau, furious that Riker has betrayed her, spills the proverbial beans, and tells them everything she knows about the skull and its effect. We quote, "The skull overwhelms you with pleasure, like a drug, until it controls you....then you become one with the will of Doshin, and you are its tool."

Naturally the first course of action is to set themselves free, and to this end Data starts removing rubble, but even for him it will take hours. Boudreau remembers a laser shovel nearby, and digs it out. They utilize it to speed their progress.

On the Enterprise Troi tells Riker that she sensed anger and confusion in Zaeb. Still confident, the commander believes that the Ferengi chose the wrong man to "mess" with. He moves over to hug her, but she is resistant, pointing out that her main concern at the moment is the problem at hand, and the fact that Captain Picard is dead.

Troi leaves the room. Meanwhile, in sickbay, Roark has come to again, and is telling Beverly of the skull and the effect it's had on Boudreau, and that she is the one who actually pushed him into the pit where he was injured. Beverly tells him what's happened, and notes, almost to herself, how Riker seems to have changed. It is Roark's opinion that the commander must be under the influence of the skull as well. Calling a private meeting between herself, Troi and Wes, Beverly explains what she's discovered and what she believes to be wrong with Number One. Bearing all the evidence in mind, perhaps the captain is still alive on the planet somewhere. Troi "tunes in" to the planet, and definitely senses life.

Let's hold it right there for a moment.

Troi may be talented and all, but this most certainly pushes the credibility of her powers. It's tough enough to believe that she can read the feelings of someone on another vessel, let alone *beneath* the surface of a planet. This makes her abilities too powerful, and sets a precedent which could work against the series in the future.

On the bridge, Riker, who suddenly seems to be growing fatigued, tells the Ferengi captain to get his people off the planet's surface immediately, because he will be demonstrating the Enterprise's power by destroying the underground city. The order is given to Worf: aim photon torpedoes at the heart of Izul.

Riker, who has apparently moved himself into Picard's quarters, sits with the skull in his hands. Worf, like everyone else, doesn't seem to question Riker's decision to destroy the underground city. He pipes in on the communication channel, reminding the commander that he's awaiting the order to fire. Riker comes out of meditation and says he'll be right there. By the time he returns to the bridge, Number One seems completely rejuvenated, and "ready to destroy." Troi approaches him, stating that this course of action may not be the right one. His only response is to smile as he turns to Worf to give the order. Troi touches his hand, appealing to his hormones, saying that they should have some time together before things start to "heat up." Agreeing, the two leave the bridge. Meanwhile, Wes has made his way into a Jeffries Tube, and sends a signal down to the planet. Boudreau picks it up on the archaeological team's communications system. Picard gets on the channel, desperately seeking information as to what's going on. The boy quickly explains, and Picard says that he and the others will get to the surface so they can be beamed aboard.

Riker and Troi, in the meantime, have gone to the captain's room, when Geordi contacts the commander, explaining that there has been unauthorized transmission from the ship. Furious, he makes his way back on to the bridge, ranting of spies running rampant aboard the Enterprise and wanting to find the person guilty of unauthorized communication. Riker orders the destruction of the city, but is interrupted by Troi's objections and contact from the Ferengi vessel, with Zaeb demanding that the Enterprise either depart this area of space or make the first move against them. The commander is delighted by the challenge.

Beverly and Wes get into the transporter room, and beam up their people just as the Kakiri Warriors are surrounding them. Riker, who is still on the bridge, is shocked when he hears Picard's voice speaking to him over the comm channel. His immediate response is that the Ferengi have cloned Picard and the others, and somehow devised a way to get them on the Enterprise without being detected. There's no choice: they must be destroyed!

Angry, Riker goes to the captain's quarters and grabs the crystal skull, which he brings with him back to the bridge. Once there, he tells Worf the crew can't be trusted, and he wants the Klingon to join him. They move into the turbolift, and Troi tells the captain, via intercom, that Riker has gone to the battle bridge, and that the situation between the Enterprise and the Ferengi vessel is heating up. Then, Geordi makes the discovery that Riker and Worf have cut off the turbo lift, essentially stranding themselves in the battle bridge, and keeping everyone else out. Picard's instinct tells him Riker is going to separate the saucer section from the rest of the ship (see the "Encounter at Farpoint" premiere episode of **The Next Generation** for full details on how this is done). The captain wants to be beamed into the battle bridge, but the operator tells him Riker has erected a force field to repel all such attempts.

On the battle bridge Riker wants Worf to separate from the saucer section, open fire on the city and prepare to engage the Ferengi vessel. Even the Klingon has some problems with this. Riker merely smiles, declaring this day will seal their destinies, and earn them each their own commands. Before Worf can respond, Picard's image appears on the main viewer. The captain desperately tries to talk Riker out of his dangerous plan. The commander tells Worf to cut off the channel, but the Klingon refuses as Picard tells Will to think for himself; to try to overcome the influence of the skull controlling him. Riker laughs this claim of outside control off, but then starts eyeing the

bag containing the skull "thirstily." Moving towards the bag, he orders Worf to open fire, but the Klingon merely asks what's in the bag. Again Riker becomes furious, trying to get past Worf to launch the photon torpedoes himself, but Worf pulls him away. Naturally the Klingon wins the struggle, until Riker grabs the skull and his strength is instantly renewed. When the skull is knocked out of his hand, Riker grabs a phaser and fires. But Worf moves too quickly, and the beam finds its mark on the skull. No sooner has the beam struck, then Riker collapses to the ground. According to the treatment, "the skull is now revealed to have a blackened, burned out core with a cracked crystal coating."

Later, on the bridge, Picard regains command, with Worf bringing him the remainders of the skull for inspection. Data's scanners indicate it no longer possesses any power. Beverly pipes in, stating that Riker is going to be okay, and firmly in control of his own mind.

As word reaches the captain that the Ferengi force has beamed back up, he orders Tasha to assemble her own people and beam down, then contacts Zaeb and firmly explains that they are on an official Federation mission, and that if any further beam down of Ferengi forces

will be seen as an act of aggression. Zaeb wants an explanation for Riker, but the captain smugly responds there's no reason to explain anything. He also mentions that they do not have the crystal skull. Zaeb considers this for a moment, flares with anger, and then Enterprise sensors detect the Ferengi vessel breaking orbit and setting off for deep space.

In sickbay, Riker regains consciousness and finds Picard, Troi, Worf and Beverly standing around him. He tries to apologize for everything that happened, but Picard says that his actions were successful in getting the Ferengi off the planet, and that in itself has to be worth something. They'll discuss everything else at a later time.

While some serious problems beset this story, "The Crystal Skull" would have made an interesting and highly effective episode of **Star Trek: The Next Generation**. Plot problems and a number of story contrivances (which could have been corrected had the writer moved to teleplay with it) exist, but there is an inherent feeling of suspense in regards to Riker. A subtle change in the commander that gradually became more pronounced as time went on, until the point where he was being fully possessed by the crystal skull, would

116

have made an interesting addition. One can only assume actor Jonathan Frakes would have welcomed the opportunity to stretch his acting abilities with this unique approach to the character of Will Riker.

This proposed view of the Ferengi would have provided a nice counter-balance to the campy way the race was portrayed in "The Last Outpost."

"SEE SPOT RUN"

Proceeding to Procyon III, the Enterprise searches for a supposed lost colony, a group of "high-tech iconoclasts" who settled the world. When the world had first been discovered, the dominant form of life was an animal known as the Rookas, a panda-like race who were not aggressive by nature, and were nearly made extinct by the settlers. The colonists trained the survivors to do various tasks, much like chimpanzees on Earth today, and bred the species on farms situated throughout the world.

An Away Team led by Riker, and including Wesley, beam down to one of the aforementioned farms, where they encounter a frightened fifteen year old girl (Delva).They eventually learn that her parents went into town to partake in an annual celebration. Wesley is

left behind with Delva as they proceed.

Picard tries to contact the Away Team, but discovers that somehow the transporter engaged a device set up by the colonists which blocks off all communication, and cut off the automatic beacon they detected as well.

Once they arrive in town, the Away Team is surprised that the settlers have reverted to a more simple lifestyle. They also see crowded book stalls and a being known as a Memory Master, who begins detailing the history of the world. Somehow the Memory Master combines and twists the history of both the planet and the Federation. Once this oration is complete, the people start throwing their books into a fire. Riker retrieves a book, and is shocked to learn that all of the pages are blank. Then, an old man named Kort takes the book from his hands, throws it into the flames and leads them to his home.

Meanwhile, Delva teaches Wes the history of Procyon III, telling him there was a time when the society flourished with technology, but then the planet was almost destroyed by the misuse of it. The people revolted against men of knowledge, and illiteracy became the norm. It is deemed better to be illiterate, than to possess the potential to destroy their world. She does, however, have

one book, which features the infamous Dick and Jane.

Kort has essentially explained the same thing to the Away Team, but adds that real books are kept hidden because they are highly illegal. History is taught by the Memory Masters, so that basic everyday knowledge will be passed from one generation to the next. At that moment, the door bursts open and the equivalent of police enter, capturing Troi, Geordi and Kort, while Riker, Data and Tasha escape. They attempt to contact the Enterprise to no avail.

According to the outline, Wesley accidentally forgets the Prime Directive (let's face it, love him or hate him, Wesley would *not* forget that directive) and reads from a Robert Frost book of poetry he just happens to carry with him. While Delva is frightened by his actually reading, she finds solace in the words spoken. Shortly thereafter, the girl's parents return. Delva explains that Wesley is a friend, and that strangers are being tried for treason. When they are alone, Wes tries to get Delva to assist him in rescuing the others.

While hiding in what's left of a scientific complex, Riker accidentally falls to a lower level, where he sees a Rooka tending books. Then he realizes these creatures are actually intelligent, and have learned to write, read and speak from association with the colonists. Naturally they fear that if such knowledge became public, they would be exterminated. They keep their abilities secret from the humans, while being drawn to a library which survives.

At their trial, Troi, Geordi and Kort are sentenced to death, with the Memory Master using a twisted version of a Federation doctrine as the reason.

The Rookas help Riker obtain "primitive weapons" which they use to get the others out of jail. Wes and Delva catch up to them, while Riker uses the Memory Master as a hostage. He tells him that if the Away Team isn't given back their weapons and communicators, then Troi will wipe the history of the planet from the Memory Master's mind. Kort steps forward with an old book of Federation codes, which the elderly Rooka reads from, including a call for "freedom of expression; freedom of worship; freedom of assembly." The people actually take these words to heart and turn against the Tribunal, demanding justice for all.

Picard manages to communicate with the Away Team and beams them back up, and while the captain reports their findings to the Federation, the elderly Rooka sits in a field on the planet, reading "Run, Spot, Run," to some children, who slowly repeat his words.

While this story would have needed work, it does present interesting concepts, most notable among them being a society that has forced itself to become illiterate rather than accidentally use knowledge to destroy itself. The ending, while effective, harkens back to "The Omega Glory" episode of the original show, where Captain Kirk reads from the Constitution of the United States in an effort to unite the Yangs and the Kohms.

"THE LEGACY"

Everyone on the bridge of the Enterprise is surprised to be picking up a radio broadcast of music. This, then, is interrupted by an emergency signal from a passenger ship which is supposedly in a "Bermuda Triangle of space." The starship approaches, but is unable to grab the vessel in its tractor beam because of an ion storm. A woman pilot named Lara volunteers to take a shuttle to the ship, which Picard allows. Unfortunately, she disappears in the storm and scanners suddenly indicate no other ship in the vicinity.

Shortly thereafter, she mysteriously returns and is debriefed by the captain. Lara reluctantly tells him she saw a beautiful winged creature outside of the shuttle. Beverly Crusher examines her, and deems her to be in perfect health. The mystery deepens, however, when the Enterprise begins sending out its own distress signal, and the crew learns that two other Federation vessels are now enroute to rescue them.

The ship starts picking up the strange music again, and the music seems to be taking control of Lara. All communication channels are suddenly jammed, and there is no way to alert the Federation or the two approaching vessels of the danger. Then Beverly's further examinations of Lara find her pregnant with a rapidly growing fetus. This was not the case before she went out in the shuttle.

As the child inside her develops, Lara grows stronger and "displays extraordinary powers," which leads Beverly to conclude that the child is superhuman. The jamming of subspace communication lessens to the point where Picard is able to contact Starfleet, who replies that they may order an abortion (No way could this have made it to the air. In Gene Roddenberry's version of the 24th Century, everything works the way it's supposed to, and an abortion definitely doesn't fit that vision). Lara, thanks to to the child, picks up signals from the broadcast they're intercepting, and warns Picard that the Enterprise is in grave danger, which can only be averted by changing the course of the starship. Picard refuses, trying to determine whether it's Lara or the alien threat speaking, but the woman convinces the navigator to follow through on her warning. The course is changed, resulting in their missing disaster.

Picard is ordered to destroy the embryo, but he offers a reason not to do so at that time. Meanwhile, Lara tells the captain that a battle between good and evil rages in a parallel universe, and the good alien wants to come into our universe to battle the evil. The child offers the key, and she wants the two of them to take a shuttlecraft. Finally, Picard "realizes that only Lara can make the decision about her future. That's the true meaning of the Prime Directive. Lara elects to go where no woman has gone before by having the child."

As the story closes, Lara takes the shuttlecraft and heads for the signal mysterious, as well as her destiny.

Again, another decent story if properly fleshed out. The idea of a rapidly developing child has already been discussed in this volume, and made it to the air in Season Two's "The Child." One can only wish this outline wasn't so short, to more clearly present the author's ideas.

"THE NEUTRAL ZONE"

Enterprise awaits the arrival of Commander Billings, a chief of security from Starfleet Command. Naturally, Tasha Yar is particularly concerned about this visit, as security has been her domain. Riker wants to know the purpose of the visit, as does Picard. Apparently Billings "wrote the book" on security, and was once an instructor at the Academy highly respected by students and peers alike. But, for the most part, the last few years of Billings life have become a mystery. He has more or less avoided the public spotlight.

Later, the Enterprise meets with the starcruiser Washington, but, for some reason, Billings (sounding very much like Bones McCoy) refuses to beam over, choosing, instead, to utilize a shuttlecraft. This accomplished, as the doors open, the crew is stunned to see Billings float out of the shuttle in what is deemed the 24th Century equivalent of a wheelchair. He is "severely disabled."

Despite being crippled at the age of 40, Billings seems very lively. Tasha asks if he will need any specific accommodations to help him physically, to which he replies in the negative. Picard requests an explanation of the nature of this mission, but Billings is not yet ready to answer, stating that all things will become clear in time. For the moment, he would like to take the "scenic-route" of the ship so that he may best determine the status of ship security. Tasha leads him off the bridge. While Riker, Geordi, Worf and Picard discuss Billings, they determine that their current heading will lead the Enterprise to the Neutral Zone, which serves as the territorial bounds between Federation space and that of the Romulans.

Billings and Tasha, meanwhile, arrive on the battle bridge, where he asks her questions regarding security, and she seems to respond appropriately. He turns the conversation to the Romulans, wanting to determine if anyone on board has had contact with that race. Before beginning her computer check, she asks if the failed Earth colony known as Davana VII (which is the world that she was rescued from) means anything to him, but he bluntly responds that Davana VII happened a long time ago, and bears no relevance to the mission at hand. Tasha is hurt, but instead of responding, chooses to work on the computer.

Tasha and Billings return to the bridge with a breakdown of people who must depart at the next starbase they come across for the duration of this mission. Worf's name is on the list, and such a suggestion infuriates Picard. Worf protests, but the captain silences him, turning to Billings and stating, quite firmly, that the crew of the Enterprise was hand-picked and they are beyond reproach. He will not transfer any of his people off, but to satisfy Billings, he will temporarily reassign Worf as Wes' tutor. While not completely happy with this decision, Billings accepts it, feeling that two security risks will be removed from the bridge. Then, Picard leads Billings into the ready room, demanding to know what in hell is going on. Finally, the man gives a response, stating that Enterprise will serve as the base for an extremely important trade conference which will be the first to include the Romulan Empire. *But* there are factions among the Romulans who would rather such an agreement not be reached. For this reason, the security of the starship is paramount. Worf, he points out, undoubtedly possesses a cultural hatred towards Romulans, and for security purposes, the Klingon should be removed. Picard bluntly points out that he himself dislikes Romulans,

and had even engaged a pair of Bird of Prey in battle several years earlier. Billings is aware of this, but notes that the battle forced the Romulans to look on the captain with respect, which is why they did not ask for the Enterprise as a location for the trade conference—they merely wanted Picard to be there.

Visiting Beverly in sickbay, Tasha asks for advice as to how she can let someone know she admires him on more than a professional level. It is the doctor's recommendation that she use the direct approach. Later, in the turbolift, Beverly runs into Billings, wanting to know why the man has refused her requests for a complete physical. He offers feeble excuses, and she turns the request into an order.

Billings comes to see Tasha in security to check on progress. As the conversation develops, Tasha notes that he is the one responsible for getting her involved in Starfleet and security work. Billings led the Starfleet security forces who rescued her and others from Davana VII, and she feels a debt toward him that can never be repaid. Surprisingly, Billings virtually ignores her, pointing out instead that the mission was nothing out of the ordinary. He then, rudely, turns the conversation back to Enterprise security, chastising her for what he's seen so

far. Security must be tightened up on the ship. He departs, leaving a stunned and hurt Tasha. Moments later Geordi and Wes enter, angered by being restricted from certain areas of the ship. Quietly, Tasha provides the explanation given her, which does not sit well with them. As the treatment notes, "Efficiency as well as harmony are beginning to suffer."

In sickbay, Beverly examines Billings, having come to the conclusion that he sustained injuries in the midst of some sort of heroic act. Billings won't talk about it. Changing the subject slightly, she points out that she and Data have been performing experiments and may be able to take nutrients from the android's spinal cord, inject them into Billings, possibly resulting in the regeneration of his "damaged nerve ends." He refuses, declaring this yet another of many attempts which raise his hopes and then destroy them when they fail. He has finally come to grips with his handicap, and learned to accept it. As the man leaves, Wes runs into him, stating that if he could have access to restricted materials located in restricted areas, he could enhance Billing's wheelchair. The man snaps back that he doesn't need anyone's help, and moves away from the boy.

The Enterprise arrives at the Neutral

Zone. Riker, sensing something amiss with Tasha, is about to ask her about it, when word comes that a Romulan ship is approaching. The ship is put on yellow alert, and Billings is requested on the bridge. The Romulan ship is hailed, and responds as Billings enters the bridge. A security officer from beams aboard, and Riker, Tasha and Data go to the transporter room to meet him. There, Sub-Commander Gar appears on the platform, immediately commenting on how primitive the Enterprise transporter is. He is escorted to the captain's ready room, where Gar explains that despite popular belief, the Empire has decided to follow through with this trade conference, although the conclusion will undoubtedly be disastrous. Gar's assignment is to ensure the Romulan delegates safety aboard the Enterprise. Picard is not happy with Gar's presence, particularly when it's been noted that he would probably love to see these talks fail.

In sickbay, Beverly asks Tasha if she thinks there might be a way to convince Billings to go through with the experiments. Tasha, still pained by her previous encounter with the man, doesn't have an answer, although she will look over the material pertaining to the experiment. Elsewhere, Gar is being given a tour of the Enterprise, to satisfy his concern over ship security.

In the ship's library, Worf delivers a lecture on Klingon history — which comes across as little more than a list of battles, but Wes is fascinated by what his tutor has to say. He also discusses a Klingon-Romulan battle, where the former proved victorious, but Gar, who has just entered the area, states that Klingon history is quite different from reality according to the Romulans. They exchange insults, and the "session" concludes with Worf noting that Klingons must be superior, as the Romulans copied their battleship design from them. This seems to quiet Gar down, as he turns his attention back to security. He wants to finish the inspection alone, to which Riker objects, but Billings notes that if the Enterprise is truly secure, then there is nothing to fear. The commander contacts Picard, while Gar adds another insult against Worf before leaving the area.

"How can someone look so much like a Vulcan, yet act like such a moron?" Worf muses.

Wes and Worf go to the transporter room, but are told by the computer that their access is denied. Wes confidently pulls out a tape recorder, and plays the captain's voice rescinding the restriction on this area. The doors open, and they enter.

This seems to be a replay of a ploy Wes used in "The Naked Now," when he used the voice of the captain to gain access to the engineering section. While some people view this as repetition of an idea, it can also be construed continuity within the series.

Wes, operating the console, beams Worf into a storage room, telling the Klingon that in five minutes he will automatically beam back. Moments later, he reappears with a variety of items.

While Gar continues his inspection, Tasha talks with Billings, with the man deducing that Doctor Crusher has requested her to speak to him. He lets her know he is aware of her memories, and expected her gratitude toward him to be warped by his handicap into something she *imagined* to be romantic. Again, she's hurt, but he insists she deal with "life's painful realities rather than dwelling on romantic memories." If nothing else, Tasha realizes that Billings has truly come to grips with remaining crippled for the rest of his life.

Gar returns to the bridge just as the vessel containing the trade delegates nears the Enterprise. He approves security measures and tells them to beam the delegates aboard, beginning with the Romulans. Riker, Data and

Tasha await their arrival in the transporter room. In mid-operation, there are a series of warning klaxons and flashing lights, and all fear the expected malfunction will beam the Romulans into the middle of space. Panic on the bridge ensues, with Gar reacting angrily to Picard. Geordi crossfeeds an alternate power source into the transporter power line, hoping it will be enough. This move, combined with Riker and Data's efforts, gets the Romulans back to their own ship safely, and the delegates want to know what happened. Picard, too, would like an answer. In the transporter room, Data removes a device from the console, noting that sabotage almost cost the lives of the delegates.

Wesley tells Picard that he used the transporter controls, although for an innocent reason. In the ready room, Worf explains exactly what he and Wes had done, confessing that he's guilty of entering a restricted area, while simultaneously stating that neither of them were involved in sabotaging the device. Gar once again reinforces how bad the idea of a trade agreement is. Picard tells Tasha to take Worf into custody until the situation can be fully investigated. When the two are alone, Worf proclaims his innocence, stating that if he

was really going to do harm to a Romulan, he would have done it face-to-face, which is the Klingon way. She is moved by his statements. Back in the ready room, Gar demands to be sent back to his ship, which Picard will happily comply with once the transporter has been repaired. Billings is angry, pointing out that he was the one who wanted Worf taken off the ship in the first place. How will the Romulans react to what has happened? Tasha contacts the ready room, requesting that everyone get ready for an image to appear on the main viewscreen.

They do so, and Tasha explains that she had kept a record of all authorized areas as well as unauthorized — which infuriates Billings, because he wasn't told. But why should she have after his reaction to everything else she had to offer? —and the computer tape shows Worf and Wes entering the transporter room. Later, the image reveals Gar entering the room as well. She calls up another image, and everyone sees Gar opening a panel and inserting a foreign object. Tasha has the image frozen.

Furious, Picard turns his attention to Gar, who "offers the Romulan equivalent of a shrug." While he admits his guilt, he attributes it to the general feeling that detente between their two people

would be a mistake. Gar, as he explains it, merely helped to speed up the natural state of things. As things develop, and with the guilty party under arrest, the trade conference continues and everyone — except Billings — seems to come out on top. Later, Billings apologizes to Tasha, but she is rather brusque with him, leaving the security office. Wes enters with schematics as well as a scale model of his idea for the man's new wheelchair. Unfortunately Billings' mind is preoccupied with Tasha.

As the Enterprise and the Romulan vessel move away from each other, Picard's log records that the trade conference was a success, and that if he's lucky, the Romulans will allow Gar to take his own life, which is that race's form of death with honor.

Later, Billings is with Beverly, studying Wes' model and voicing his approval of it. If it's alright with the boy, he would like to give the design to Federation researchers so that it can be developed for practical use throughout their territory. Beverly thinks this would be fine, but why not allow the boy to develop the first unit for him? Billings coyly notes that he had hoped he wouldn't need it. Shortly thereafter, both Billings and Data are on adjoining tables in sickbay, and Beverly conducts the operation discussed earlier.

Still later, on the main bridge, everyone is at their post, with Enterprise enroute to meet with Billings' ship. Suddenly, there's another emergency. Enterprise has to deliver dilithium crystals to an "out-of-the-way" starbase, and the new course is laid in. At that moment, Billings *walks* in, a cane in his hand. Everyone is delighted. Billings, who is pleased beyond words, approaches Tasha and asks if she could possibly join him for dinner, as he has learned that solitude degrees can have nothing but a damaging effect on a person's humanity. Without responding to the man, Tasha receives permission from Picard to leave the bridge. Billings offers her his arm, and the two approach the turbolift, with Picard noting that they will have to detour to Gorn space for a short while. Billings replies that there is no rush, as he and Tasha enter the turbolift.

Despite basic elements of this reminding one of the original show's "Journey to Babel," "The Neutral Zone" would have made a wonderful episode of **The Next Generation**. There's plenty of mystery, strong character development and a neat twist in the form of internal conflict between the main players. Worf, in particular, is handled nicely, even though his racial intolerance of Gar might not be deemed correct by the producers. Most importantly, everything about this story rang true-to-life, and it is truly unfortunate that it was not taken further. Season Two, in particular, could have used a story like this one. Incidentally, writer Greg Strangis moved over to Paramount's **War of the Worlds**, where he served as producer.

A LETTER TO THE NEXT GENERATION
FROM GENE RODDENBERRY, THE CREATOR OF STAR TREK
[FROM THE PRESS KIT FOR STAR TREK: THE NEXT GENERATION]

Good wishes from a television dramatist who lived a hundred years before your time. I create science fiction tales set in your 21st Century and beyond for television and movie audiences. These are tales which reflect the affection and optimism I have for the human creature. I welcome this opportunity to share my perspectives with you.

For many living now, today is a time of fear and even despair. Some believe that life has become too complex for us. Or too artificial. Or that this era's nuclear missiles, its waves of hysterical nationalism or quarreling superstitions mean a violent end for the human creature, perhaps as soon as the close of our present century.

I believe the complete opposite to be true. The present tumult in our world is the natural and understandable result of a vigorous intelligence moving out of the savagery of our lifeform's childhood. Instead of humanity's demise, our era seems to be filled with evidence that we were meant to survive and evolve much further.

For example, a recent flood of remarkable human happenings include a primal invention as revolutionary as the discovery of fire, the wheel and language. We call it the *computer*, an astonishing device which handles information at near-light speed and in ways suggests humanity has been gifted with the perfect servant. Next, largely because of the computer, we have begun to recognize that the human brain is an equally astonishing device whose ten *billion* or so neurons appear to interconnect into a potential of *trillions* of thought patterns. Rather than being unable to handle the complexities of today, the combination of computer and brain appears to be doubling human knowledge every six or seven years, leading us toward knowledge and ability our ancestors would have considered godlike.

Which means that the human future is not for the fainthearted. The most dramatic happening in our era has been our first efforts to move out from our home planet. Our first moon visits are remarkably similar to the early sailing craft that visited the American New World. Bold children, both! Those early sea voyages found a wilderness as forbidding to them as the moon's landscape seemed to us much later on.

I find it equally remarkable that, so far, no other intelligent life forms seem to exist on those worlds overhead. In fact, everything about our sun and its planets proclaims "RESERVED FOR HUMANITY." What a lovely educational arrangement for the offspring of our fertile Earth-egg planet! Having left childhood behind as we move out from our home planet, humanity is ready for the stretching and learning of adolescence.

What better place to evolve into adulthood than in our own solar system? There exists, out in our own "backyard," an incredible treasure house of eight other planets, plus dozens of moons and other raw material —plus the almost inexhaustible energy of our hydrogen furnace sun with which to shape those materials to our needs.

All of which makes it interesting that the galaxy's other stars are, for now, inconceivably distant. Even traveling at light speed, most range from thousands to millions of years away. In its own way, this fact is as heartening as the apparent absence of other intelligent life on the worlds circling our own star. If our universe is a gigantic life and intelligence-creating machine as some believe, what better way of protecting life forms than a system of natural laws which protects them from one another until they become adult and capable of understanding the master plan?

One obstacle to adulthood needs to be solved immediately: we must learn not just to accept differences between ourselves and our ideas, but to enthusiastically welcome and enjoy them. Diversity contains as many treasures as those waiting for us on other worlds. We will find it impossible to fear diversity and to enter the future at the same time.

If the future is not for the fainthearted, it is even more certainly not for the cowardly. One of the saddest spectacles of our time is to watch the leaders of Earth's nations meeting together clumsily and embarrassedly, exchanging slogans containing grains of friendship and understanding, yet fearful that this might constitute some awful blasphemy. Those who insist theirs is the only correct government or economic system deserve the same contempt as those who insist that they have the only true God.

As I began by saying, I am a television dramatist who lived many years before your time, and I realize that the future will be infinitely more complex than anything I am able to imagine. I hope, however, that by your time some small truths will be found in the rough sketch of tomorrow that I offer here. If not, at least you may find this a pleasant and entertaining tale.

The preceding was taken from "In 'Open Forum'" sponsored by Volkswagon and appearing second in a series in Time Magazine.

THE COUCH POTATO BOOK CATALOG 5715 N BALSAM, LAS VEGAS, NV 89130

THE FREDDY KRUEGER STORY

The making of the monster. Including interviews with director Wes Craven and star Robert Englund. Plus an interview with Freddy himself! $14.95

THE ALIENS STORY

Interviews with movie director James Cameron, stars Sigourney Weaver and Michael Biehn and effects people and designers Ron Cobb, Syd Mead, Doug Beswick and lots more!...$14.95

ROBOCOP

Law enforcement in the future. Includes interviews with the stars, the director, the writer, the special effects people, the storyboard artists and the makeup men! $16.95

MONSTERLAND'S HORROR IN THE '80s

The definitive book of the horror films of the '80s. Includes interviews with the stars and makers of Aliens, Freddy Krueger, Robocop, Predator, Fright Night, Terminator and all the others! $17.95

LOST IN SPACE

THE COMPLEAT LOST IN SPACE
244 PAGES...$17.95
TRIBUTE BOOK
Interviews with everyone!...$7.95
TECH MANUAL
Technical diagrams to all of the special ships and devices plus exclusive production artwork....$9.95

GERRY ANDERSON

SUPERMARIONATION
Episode guides and character profiles to Capt Scarlet, Stingray, Fireball, Thunderbirds, Supercar and more...240 pages...$17.95

BEAUTY AND THE BEAST

THE UNOFFICIAL BEAUTY&BEAST
Complete first season guide including interviews and biographies of the stars. 132 pages $14.95

DARK SHADOWS

DARK SHADOWS TRIBUTE BOOK
Interviews, scripts and more... 160 pages...$14.95

DARK SHADOWS INTERVIEWS BOOK
A special book interviewing the entire cast. $18.95

DOCTOR WHO THE BAKER YEARS

A complete guide to Tom Baker's seasons as the Doctor including an in-depth episode guide, interviews with the companions and profiles of the characters... 300 pages...$19.95

THE DOCTOR WHO ENCYCLOPEDIA: THE FOURTH DOCTOR

Encyclopedia of every character, villain and monster of the Baker Years. ..240 pages...$19.95

THE COUCH POTATO BOOK CATALOG 5715 N BALSAM, LAS VEGAS, NV 89130

Boring, but Necessary Ordering Information!

Payment: All orders must be prepaid by check or money order. Do not send cash. All payments must be made in US funds only.

Shipping: We offer several methods of shipment for our product.

Postage is as follows:

For books priced under $10.00— for the first book add $2.50. For each additional book under $10.00 add $1.00. (This is per individual book priced under $10.00, not the order total.)

For books priced over $10.00— for the first book add $3.25. For each additional book over $10.00 add $2.00. (This is per individual book priced over $10.00, not the order total.)

These orders are filled as quickly as possible. Sometimes a book can be delayed if we are temporarily out of stock. You should note on your order whether you prefer us to ship the book as soon as available or send you a merchandise credit good for other TV goodies or send you your money back immediately. Shipments normally take 2 or 3 weeks, but allow up to12 weeks for delivery.

Special UPS 2 Day Blue Label RUSH SERVICE: Special service is available for desperate Couch Potatos. These books are shipped within 24 hours of when we receive your order and should take 2 days to get from us to you.

For the first **RUSH SERVICE** book under $10.00 add $4.00. For each additional l book under $10.00 and $1.25. (This is per individual book priced under $10.00, not the order total.)

For the first **RUSH SERVICE** book over $10.00 add $6.00. For each additional book over $10.00 add $3.50 per book. (This is per individual book priced over $10.00, not the order total.)

Canadian and Foreign shipping rates are the same except that Blue Label RUSH SERVICE is not available. All Canadian and Foreign orders are shipped as books or printed matter.

DISCOUNTS! DISCOUNTS! Because your orders are what keep us in business we offer a discount to people that buy a lot of our books as our way of saying thanks. On orders over $25.00 we give a 5% discount. On orders over $50.00 we give a 10% discount. On orders over $100.00 we give a 15% discount. On orders over $150.00 we give a 20% discount. Please list alternates when possible. Please state if you wish a refund or for us to backorder an item if it is not in stock.

100% satisfaction guaranteed. We value your support. You will receive a full refund as long as the copy of the book you are not happy with is received back by us in reasonable condition. No questions asked, except we would like to know how we failed you. Refunds and credits are given as soon as we receive back the item you do not want.

Please have mercy on Phyllis and carefully fill out this form in the neatest way you can. Remember, she has to read a lot of them every day and she wants to get it right and keep you happy! You may use a duplicate of this order blank as long as it is clear. **Please don't forget to include payment! And remember, we *love* repeat friends...**

■■■■■■■■■■■■■■■■■■■■■■■■■■ORDER FORM■■■■■■■■■■■■■■■■■■■■■■■■■■■■■■■

_____The Phantom $16.95
_____The Green Hornet $16.95
_____The Shadow $16.95
_____Flash Gordon Part One $16.95_____Part Two $16.95
_____Blackhawk $16.95
_____Batman $16.95
_____The UNCLE Technical Manual One $9.95 _____Two $9.95
_____The Green Hornet Television Book $14.95
_____Number Six The Prisoner Book $14.95
_____The Wild Wild West $17.95
_____Trek Year One $10.95
_____Trek Year Two $12.95
_____Trek Year Three $12.95
_____The Animated Trek $14.95
_____The Movies $12.95
_____Next Generation $19.95
_____The Lost Years $14.95
_____The Trek Encyclopedia $19.95
_____Interviews Aboard The Enterprise $18.95
_____The Ultimate Trek $75.00
_____Trek Handbook $12.95_____Trek Universe $17.95
_____The Crew Book $17.95
_____The Making of the Next Generation $14.95
_____The Freddy Krueger Story $14.95
_____The Aliens Story $14.95
_____Robocop $16.95
_____Monsterland's Horror in the '80s $17.95
_____The Compleat Lost in Space $17.95
_____Lost in Space Tribute Book $9.95
_____Lost in Space Tech Manual $9.95
_____Supermarionation $17.95
_____The Unofficial Beauty and the Beast $14.95
_____Dark Shadows Tribute Book $14.95
_____Dark Shadows Interview Book $18.95
_____Doctor Who Baker Years $19.95
_____The Doctor Who Encyclopedia:The 4th Doctor $19.95
_____Illustrated Stephen King $12.95
_____Gunsmoke Years $14.95

NAME:_____

STREET:_____

CITY:_____

STATE:_____

ZIP:_____

TOTAL:_____ SHIPPING_____

**SEND TO: COUCH POTATO,INC.
5715 N BALSAM, LAS VEGAS, NV 89130**

EXCITING EARLY ISSUES!

If your local comic book specialty store no longer has copies of the early issues you may want to order them directly from us.

By Roy Crane:
_Buz Sawyer #1 _Buz Sawyer #2 _Buz Sawyer #3 _Buz Sawyer #4 _Buz Sawyer #5

By Alex Raymond:
_Jungle Jim 1_Jungle Jim 2_Jungle Jim 3_Jungle Jim 4 _Jungle Jim 5 _Jungle Jim 6 _Jungle Jim 7
_Rip Kirby #1 _Rip Kirby #2 _Rip Kirby #3 _Rip Kirby #4

By Lee Falk and Phil Davis:
_Mandrake #1_Mandrake #2_Mandrake #3_Mandrake #4 _Mandrake #5 _Mandrake #6 _Mandrake #7

By Peter O'Donnell and Jim Holdaway:
_Modesty1 _Modesty 2_Modesty 3_Modesty 4_Modesty 5 _Modesty#6 _Modesty#7
_Modesty ANNUAL ($5.00)

By Hal Foster:
_P V #1 _P V #2 _P V #3 _P V #4 _P V #5 _P V #6 _P V #7 _P V #8 _P V AN. ($5.00)

By Archie Goodwin and Al Williamson:
_Secret Agent #1 _Secret Agent #2_Secret Agent #3 _Secret Agent #4 _Secret Agent #5 _Secret Agent #6

(All about the heroes including interviews with Hal Foster, Lee Falk and Al Williamson:)
___ THE KING COMIC HEROES $14.95
(The following two book-size collections preserve the original strip format)
___ THE MANDRAKE SUNDAYS $14.95
___ **THE PHANTOM SUNDAYS $14.95**

___ (Enclosed) Please enclose $3.00 per comic ordered
and/or $17.95 for THE KING COMIC HEROES
and/or $14.95 for THE MANDRAKE SUNDAYS.
and/or $14.95 for THE PHANTOM SUNDAYS.
Shipping and handling are included.

Name: _ _ _ _ _ _ _ _ _ _ _ _ _ _ _

Street: _ _ _ _ _ _ _ _ _ _ _ _ _ _ _

City: _ _ _ _ _ _ _ _ _ _ _ _ _ _ _ _

State: _ _ _ _ _ _ _ _ _ _ _ _ _ _ _

Zip   Code: _ _ _ _ _ _ _ _ _ _
Check or money order only. No cash please. All payments must be in US funds. Please add $5.00 to foreign orders.
I remembered to enclose:$_ _ _ _ _
Please send to:
Pioneer, 5715 N. Balsam Rd., Las Vegas, NV 89130